## By Shelley Shepard Gray

### Sisters of the Heart series
*Hidden • Wanted • Forgiven • Grace*

### Seasons of Sugarcreek series
*Winter's Awakening • Spring's Renewal*
*Autumn's Promise • Christmas in Sugarcreek*

### Families of Honor series
*The Caregiver • The Protector • The Survivor*
*A Christmas for Katie (novella)*

### The Secrets of Crittenden County series
*Missing • The Search • Found • Peace*

### The Days of Redemption series
*Daybreak • Ray of Light • Eventide • Snowfall*

### Return to Sugarcreek series
*Hopeful • Thankful • Joyful*

### Amish Brides of Pinecraft series
*The Promise of Palm Grove • The Proposal at Siesta Key*
*A Wedding at the Orange Blossom Inn*
*A Wish on Gardenia Street (novella)*
*A Christmas Bride in Pinecraft*

### The Charmed Amish Life series
*A Son's Vow • A Daughter's Dream*

### Other books
*Redemption*

# A Daughter's Dream

# A Daughter's Dream

## THE CHARMED AMISH LIFE, BOOK TWO

Shelley Shepard Gray

AVON
INSPIRE
*An Imprint of* HarperCollins*Publishers*

P.S.™ is a trademark of HarperCollins Publishers.

HarperCollins books may be purchased for educational, business, or sales promotional use. For information please e-mail the Special Markets Department at SPsales@harpercollins.com.

FIRST EDITION

*Designed by Diahann Sturge*

*Illustrated map copyright © 2015 by Laura Hartman Maestro*

Library of Congress Cataloging-in-Publication Data has been applied for.

ISBN 978-0-06-233781-8

16 17 18 19 20    OV/RRD    10 9 8 7 6 5 4 3 2 1

To Laura Klynstra, Abby, and Steve. Thank
you for bringing my book to life!

The author is grateful for being allowed to reprint the Granola Bars
recipe from Country Blessings Cookbook by Clara Coblentz.
The Shrock's Homestead
9943 Copperhead Rd. N.W.
Sugarcreek, OH 44681

Be of good courage and do it.

Ezra 10:4

If we fill our houses with regrets of yesterday and worries of tomorrow, we have no today for which to be thankful.

Amish proverb, from *Country Blessings Cookbook*

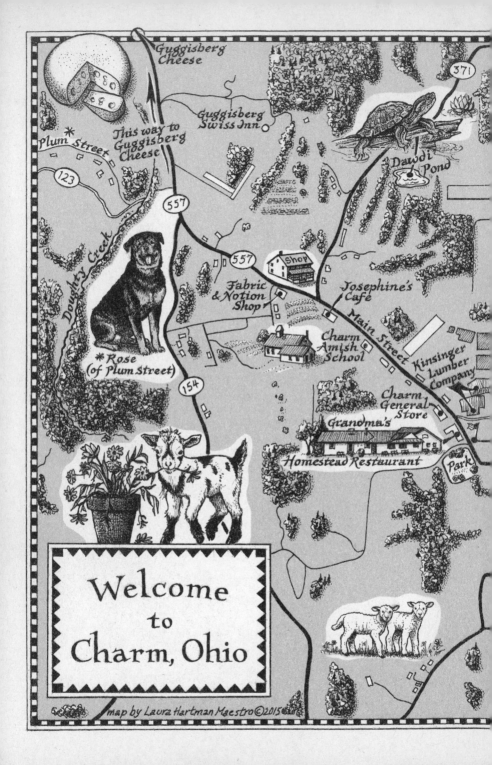

Guggisberg Cheese

This way to Guggisberg Cheese

Plum Street

123

Guggisberg Swiss Inn

371

Dawdi Pond

557

557

Shop

Doughty Creek

Fabric & Notion Shop

Josephine's Cafe

Main Street

Rose (of Plum Street)

154

Charm Amish School

Kinsinger Lumber Company

Charm General Store

Grandma's Homestead Restaurant

Park

Welcome to Charm, Ohio

map by Laura Hartman Maestro ©2015

371

369

157

369 the Kinsinger Home

157

Oscar

Simon's House

159

Charm Public School

Bank

70

U.S. Post Office

70

Darla's Farm

557

600

159

Walnut Creek

Many of these locations are real, but like Princess the goat and Oscar the bulldog, Shelley imagined a few, too.

# Chapter 1

*Thursday, August 13*

Keeping twenty-five schoolchildren reasonably happy and on task for a solid hour was harder than it looked.

As Rebecca Kinsinger stood at the front of the classroom and eyed the group of students staring right back at her, she realized she had seriously misjudged her ability to manage small children.

In the last hour, the twenty-five students, ranging in ages from five to fourteen, had decidedly taken the upper hand. They'd talked to one another. They'd ignored her wishes. They didn't seem all that interested in the work their usual teacher had assigned them to do. Even the four children whom she knew well were acting up. Evan, Samuel, Maisie, and Gretel Kurtz acted as if they had forgotten that their elder sister, Darla, was married to Rebecca's brother Lukas.

It seemed that different rules applied at school than when they visited her home.

As she watched a pair of girls pass notes to each other, Rebecca didn't even bother to intervene. She was coming to the conclusion that the only thing the students did seem rather excited about was the approach of the end of the school day.

In fifteen minutes' time, to be exact.

She was starting to get excited about the end of the day, too.

As the low murmur of voices grew louder by tiny degrees with each passing minute, Rebecca decided that she didn't blame Rachel Mast, the students' teacher, for taking her time returning. Rachel had needed Rebecca's help watching her class because she had a doctor's appointment, but being alone with this bunch for eight hours at a time would make anyone yearn for a break.

As two sweet-looking girls sitting in the middle of the first row started giggling to each other, Rebecca knew that it was time to regain control. Otherwise, Rachel would never let her help out in her classroom again, and Rebecca really wanted to learn how to be a good teacher.

She clapped her hands lightly. "*Kinner*, please. All of you have assignments to complete. It is time to get busy and work."

After a pause, about half of them quieted and settled into their assignments. Two of the oldest boys, however, merely stared at her.

When it became apparent that neither of them was in any hurry to mind her, she wove her way through the row of desks until she stood directly in front of them. "I was talking to you boys as well."

The sandy-haired boy smirked. "Oh. I wasna sure, 'cause no one's called me a child for well on two years."

"You might not be a small child but you are certainly not a

grown-up." She placed her hands on her hips and fastened her eyes on him. "Now get busy."

The boy picked up his pencil, but his friend, whom Rebecca knew to be Peter Schlabach, folded his arms across his chest. "I'll do it later," Peter said. Then he lifted his chin, practically daring her to argue with his pronouncement.

Ack, but this was terrible! Why were the men at her family's lumber mill always polite and amiable to her but these . . . these *kinner* were not? Unable to stop herself, she glanced at Evan and Samuel. They looked as if they were trying hard to act like they didn't know her.

Attempting to look far more sure of herself than she felt, Rebecca said, "Peter, you'd best get to work. I know Mrs. Mast expects you to do it now."

"I'll talk to her when she gets back." With a shrug, he added, "I'm almost done with school, anyway. I'm fourteen. I'm already working part time at the mill, you know."

Oh, she knew. Rebecca figured everyone in Charm knew of Peter Schlabach. He'd been a handful when he was five, and the last nine years hadn't changed him much—unless he was at the mill. There, he became a completely different person. He was respectful and hardworking. Polite and modest.

Her older brother Lukas loved him. Lukas's best friend, Simon, did, too. They were constantly teasing Peter or giving him some special errand to do because he was such a hard worker.

But here at school?

She had yet to see any of those qualities.

Perhaps it was time to try a little less patience and a little more steel. Stiffening her spine, she said, "Peter, you might be all of fourteen but you are still a student in this class. That means you need to be respectful and follow directions."

But instead of being cowed, Peter got to his feet. Even at fourteen, the boy was several inches taller than she was. "*Jah*, but you ain't my teacher, Miss Kinsinger. Only my boss's sister."

At a loss for words, Rebecca blinked. His harsh tone took her aback. Just as she was debating whether to remind him that she would not hesitate to share this other side of his personality with her brother, the door opened.

"That's enough, Peter," Rachel said sternly as she walked down the center aisle of the one-room schoolhouse. "Sit down and apologize to Miss Kinsinger."

Peter complied immediately. "I am sorry, Miss Kinsinger."

It was hard to come to terms with the transformation that had come about before her eyes. Peter's cocky bravado went into hiding. All at once, he looked exactly like he did at the mill: a strong boy who'd grown up doing chores and had a lifetime of hard work awaiting him.

"No harm done," she said weakly.

"Hmmph," Rachel said. Standing in front of her students, she placed her hands on her hips. The room went silent. "Scholars, I am most displeased by what I am seeing. I expect you all to behave much better when Miss Kinsinger is here."

All the students looked shamefaced.

Rebecca was so amazed by their reactions, she moved to stand against the wall and simply watched as Rachel competently walked up and down the rows, reviewing homework assignments. Every so often, she would touch a child's shoulder or point to the paper he or she was working on. She never raised her voice. She was gentle and kind, yet firm.

She was a marvel.

As she spoke, the children wrote notes in their assignment booklets, gathered papers and textbooks, and generally acted like every word she said was the most important thing each had ever heard.

When she returned to the front of the classroom, Rachel smiled brightly. "*Kinner*, it's time to go home. Gather your lunch pails and backpacks, stack your chairs, and line up."

Again, each task was done immediately and with care. Five minutes later, Rebecca watched Rachel walk to the door, open it wide, and dismiss the class. She smiled at each one, gave hugs to a couple of the little girls, and spoke softly to Peter.

When the last of the students were gone, Rachel turned to Rebecca and smiled. "*Danke* for helping me today, Rebecca. You were a lifesaver."

The praise was as embarrassing as it was unwarranted. "I don't think that was the case at all, Rachel. I tried my best, but chaos reigned. I don't know what happened—I was sure I could manage things easily for an hour."

She chuckled. "Don't fret. You did fine. It's simply in children's natures to stretch their boundaries. They like to push a bit, just to see when someone will push right back."

"Well, they certainly pushed." They also won. Again, Rebecca wondered how it was possible for her to work so well with hundreds of grown men at the lumber mill but be putty in twenty-five children's hands. "I see I have a lot to learn about managing a classroom."

Rachel waved off her concerns. "Don't be so hard on yourself. Any job takes time to learn. I'm sure I would be a nervous wreck managing things like you do at the mill. Whenever I've come to visit Marcus, I've seen you at your desk, surrounded by demanding men and ringing telephones." She shivered dramatically. "Give me children to manage any day."

"That's nothing. All it took was practice." Hearing her own words, Rebecca grinned. "I guess I just need some more practice with the children."

"You do, especially if you are serious about wanting to take on this job one day."

"I am serious. But I don't want your job," she assured her quickly. "Simply a teaching job at one of the Amish schools in the area."

"If that is what you want to do, I'm sure you will succeed just fine," Rachel said. "I've never seen you back down or give up in all the years I've known ya."

That was a nice compliment. Rebecca hoped Rachel was right in this case. She'd had a dream of being a teacher for years, but had never been able to give it much attention because of the demands of the mill.

However, after last year's terrible accident at the lumberyard, which had killed five men, including her father, Rebecca had decided the time had come to stop putting dreams off and start putting them into practice. It was simply too bad that her first opportunity to be in charge of the classroom had gone so badly.

Not wanting to dwell on herself anymore, she looked at Rachel closely. "Did everything go all right with your appointment?"

"*Jah.*" A small, secret smile appeared on Rachel's face before vanishing.

Just as Rebecca was about to ask what that smile had been about, a man appeared at the door, his hand resting on the

shoulder of a shy-looking thirteen- or fourteen-year-old girl.
"Excuse me. Is one of you the teacher?"

While Rebecca found herself staring rather dumbly at the
man who was entirely too handsome to be any teenager's parent,
Rachel lifted one of her hands. "I am," she said in a sweet voice.
"I'm Rachel Mast."

"Hi," the newcomer said with a tentative smile. He was a bit
older than Rebecca, and was wearing a long-sleeved light green
shirt and heavy boots peeking out from beneath his dark trousers. Rebecca also noticed his mesmerizing green eyes.

After squeezing the girl's shoulder once, he dropped his hand.
"My name is Jacob Yoder and this here is Lilly," he said a bit
awkwardly. "I need to enroll her in school."

Rachel smiled at the girl.

As did Rebecca. Looking at the teenager, Rebecca noticed
that she, too, had green eyes. But instead of dark brown hair like
Jacob, she had dark auburn. She also seemed to be blessed with
skin that tanned instead of freckled. She was a pretty girl who
was going to be beautiful one day.

"Hiya, Lilly," Rachel said in her sweet way. "Like I said, I'm
Rachel Mast, the teacher here at Charm School."

"Hi," Lilly said. She met Rachel's eyes briefly before looking
down at her tennis-shoe-clad feet.

"Did you just move here?" Rebecca asked. Though she didn't
know every Amish family in Charm, she recognized most.

"I just arrived here from Florida," the man said.

"Welcome to Charm, then," Rachel said easily. "This is my
friend Rebecca Kinsinger. She volunteers here from time to
time."

Feeling a bit tongue-tied, Rebecca lifted a hand. "Hiya."

Jacob glanced her way, then stilled. "Hi. It's, ah, it's nice to meet you," Jacob said.

Rebecca belatedly realized she was probably smiling so broadly that the dimple in her right cheek was showing.

When he didn't add anything else, either about himself or Lilly, Rachel cleared her throat. "Rebecca's family owns the lumber mill. Do you work there?"

"*Nee*. I'm a farmer."

Still looking at her feet, Lilly smiled for the first time.

When Jacob noticed her expression, he laughed. "Lilly's smiling because I'm currently not much of a farmer. I keep making mistakes right and left. We just moved in with my parents, Lilly's grandparents. I'm afraid farming is as unfamiliar to me as building houses in the Florida heat would be for most of the men around here."

"Someone recently told me to have patience with my wishes and dreams," Rebecca ventured, unable to keep from smiling at him. "Maybe that would work for you in this case, too?"

"I hope so." He smiled back at her. "My *daed* is counting on my help."

"I bet you both will get the hang of things here in Ohio in no time," Rachel said. "Things are different from Florida, for sure, but the people are just as nice. Everyone helps each other, just like always."

"Only *he* needs to get the hang of things here," Lilly said, slowly coming out of her shell. "I've been living in Ohio. I was just over in Berlin."

Just as Rebecca was going to ask why they'd been living in two different places, Rachel said smoothly, "How about the two of you come sit down? I have some paperwork you'll need to fill out before tomorrow's class."

"What kind of paperwork?" Lilly asked. "Is it a test?"

"Nothing of the sort," Rachel said. "I simply need some basic information. We'll worry about schoolwork and figuring out where you'll fit in best tomorrow."

Jacob nodded. "That sounds like a plan. Now, what time should Lilly get here? Seven thirty? Eight?"

Feeling like she was in the way, Rebecca gathered her things. "I'll be seeing you, Rachel. You know where to find me if you need my help."

"It was good to meet you, Rebecca," Jacob said.

She felt her cheeks heat. Seeking to cover it, she smiled more brightly. "*Danke.* It was *gut* to meet the both of you."

"See you soon, Becky," Rachel said before turning her full attention toward the man and the teenager.

It seemed to be another indication of Rachel's expertise in the classroom. In less than an hour, Rachel had returned from a doctor's appointment, taken back control of her class, counseled Rebecca, and was now greeting a new student and her father. She was able to manage multiple tasks easily and accept transitions with hardly a blink of the eye.

Rebecca, on the other hand, was juggling a dozen questions about the students, asking herself how she could have done things better, and wondering why Lilly hadn't been living with her father until recently.

Rebecca stewed on all that had transpired that morning as she walked down the short sidewalk toward Main Street. It was time to go back to Kinsinger Lumber, where she usually worked at the reception desk eight hours of the day. Today it would only be for a few hours, but it was sure to be busy. She'd be lucky to have a minute to grab a cup of coffee.

But she was so rattled by her day, and her reaction to Jacob Yoder, she decided that she needed that cup of coffee as soon as possible. Maybe even a slice of pie, too. Anything to delay her return to work. So, she turned left on Main instead of right. In no time at all, she was standing in front of Josephine's Café.

When she saw Darla waving at her from one of the brightly painted tables next to the window, Rebecca grinned and entered quickly. Darla had recently married her brother Lukas. Before then, she'd been a close friend of the family for as long as Rebecca could remember.

"Darla, seeing you through the window was a nice surprise."

"It's nice to see you, too," Darla answered with a happy smile. "Lukas had a light load of meetings today, so he decided to leave early. I told him I'd wait for him here." Pointing to her half-filled plate resting on a red gingham placemat, she said, "Josephine made fresh apple-spice cake with cream-cheese frosting."

"Oh, that's one of my favorites." Looking around, Rebecca debated whether she had time to get a slice or not. "So, how was work today?"

"Pretty *gut*. Since I now only work at the post office three days a week, I enjoy my time there. Where have you been? You're usually at work this time of day."

"Rachel Mast had an appointment, so I was volunteering over at the school today."

"And? How did it go?" Darla knew how much Rebecca wanted to be a teacher.

"Not well. At all. Actually, I pretty much embarrassed myself in front of Rachel. I simply don't know if I'm cut out for teaching."

"*Kaffi*, Rebecca?" Josephine, the proprietor, asked.

"*Jah*. Please," she added, deciding work could wait awhile longer.

"And cake?"

She couldn't resist. "*Jah*. You'd best bring me a slice, too."

After Josephine moved away, Darla studied Rebecca more closely. "Now, why do you think you're not cut out for teaching?"

"If I told you all the reasons, you'd be here until morning."

Darla laughed. "Becky, listen to you," she said, using the nickname most everyone used. "I'm sure it wasn't that bad."

"*Nee*, it was." Taking a deep breath, Rebecca forced herself to share what she was really thinking. "Maybe teaching isn't for me. Maybe I need to listen to my brother and be happy with what I have—a good job with our family's business."

Darla chuckled. "As much as I would like to say Lukas is always right, we both know that ain't the case."

Josephine brought Rebecca a generous slice of apple cake and coffee and freshened Darla's cup.

Rebecca took a fortifying sip, then added two heaping spoonfuls of sugar and a liberal dose of cream. "Does Lukas know that you talk like this about him?"

She was teasing, of course. Lukas loved Darla, and pretty much always had. But as far as she knew, Darla had always been a proponent of everything Lukas said and did. So, to hear Darla offer a quip like that was a little off-putting.

"I've known my husband almost as long as you have, Becky. We've also locked horns a time or two. Or twenty. Bickering seems to work for us."

"I know." It was odd, but Darla and Lukas did seem to thrive on teasing each other and debating most everything.

Rebecca had never wanted a relationship like that. No, if she ever found the right man, she was sure he was going to be easygoing and calm. And kind, too.

Suddenly, she found herself thinking about Jacob Yoder again. He was tall and handsome, but didn't come across as imposing. Instead, he had seemed like he would be easy to talk to. He had certainly been easy to look at.

Slightly appalled by the direction of her thoughts, she turned to gaze out the window. Given her track record, she wondered if she was even destined to have a relationship. So far, none of the men she'd casually dated had struck any kind of spark.

To be fair, she didn't think the problem had as much to do with the men as with herself. Though she'd never dared admit it to anyone, Rebecca's heart and soul had taken a tumble over the years. It wasn't easy to lose both parents. Then, just a couple of weeks ago, her little brother, Levi, had left Charm, saying he needed a couple of months to mourn and adjust to all the changes that had taken place in their family.

She understood but she'd also taken his leaving hard. It was starting to feel like the people she loved weren't going to stick around anymore.

Sipping her coffee, she wondered how to admit all of that, and if she even should, when she noticed Darla's posture completely change. Honestly, it was as if a light bulb had just illuminated inside her.

"Ah, here comes Lukas," Darla said with a smile.

On cue, the door to the café swung open and in walked Rebecca's big brother.

Even though she was his sister, Rebecca didn't wonder why Darla lit up when she saw him. Lukas Kinsinger was eye-catching. Over six feet tall, he was finely muscled and sported clear bluish-gray eyes, closely cropped strawberry-blond hair, and a constant tan. He was handsome, very handsome.

But what really was mesmerizing was his take-charge personality. Lukas was the type of man who led others. He was confident and cool and never let anyone tell him what to do. He was a natural-born leader, and people loved to follow him. They always had.

Except maybe petite Darla. She loved to banter with him.

"Hiya, Darla," he murmured. "Sorry I'm late. A couple of managers were having some problems. I needed to stay around and help as much as I could."

Darla beamed. "I understand. Plus, I got to have a moment to chat with Rebecca."

Turning to her, Lukas nodded his head. "Hey, Becky. It's *gut* to see ya . . . but I thought you were going to go back to work after you volunteered at the school?"

"I was on my way when I saw Darla through the window. I stopped in to say hello, then decided to keep her company until you got here." Though that wasn't really the truth, she knew Lukas wouldn't point out that Josephine's Café was in the opposite direction of the mill.

"I'm glad she did, too," Darla said. "I wanted to hear about her time at the school."

"Did it go all right?" Lukas asked.

"*Jah*," Rebecca answered with a tiny wink Darla's way. There was no way she was going to admit all the problems she had to Lukas. He'd try to make her stop volunteering. "Well enough."

"Oh. *Gut.*" Turning back to his wife, Lukas softened his tone. "You ready to go home now? We should probably give Amelia a hand." Turning to Rebecca, he said, "I think she was going to make some casseroles for the Wood family this afternoon. They have new twins, you know."

Darla immediately got to her feet. "Of course. Maybe we can even deliver the casseroles for her, or I can work on supper so she can get some time out of the house."

"Either option sounds good, Darla. Whatever you and Amelia want to do." Glancing in Rebecca's direction, his voice turned no-nonsense again. "Becky, I left a stack of invoices and letters. Could you take care of the most urgent ones before you go home?"

"Sure. I'll ask Josephine to wrap my snack to go."

"*Danke*. Don't worry about paying. I'll take care of it."

After claiming a white paper bag and to-go cup from Jo, Rebecca was on her way. " See you later." She took two steps toward the door before she turned around. "Hey, Luke? Who's in charge this afternoon?" She hated asking that. A year ago, their father had always been in charge. More recently, Levi had been in charge when Lukas left for the day. Now other men outside the family had started to step in.

"Simon." His voice was noticeably cooler, illustrating that he, too, was having just as hard a time with their brother's abrupt departure from Charm.

"*Danke*. All right, then. I'm off to the mill," she called out as she rushed through the door.

There was a very good possibility that she was going to be working late tonight. She didn't mind, though. Actually, she was starting to think that maybe she needed the reminder of what was constant in her life.

Her parents might have died far too young, her brother might have taken off with little notice for parts unknown, and she might not necessarily like being around men who worked for her brother and were therefore undatable—but she could count on her job. And that, she was discovering in her upside-down life, meant a whole lot.

# Chapter 2

*That same day*

Jacob's father greeted him and Lilly at the door with a bright smile. "So, how did your visit to your new school go?"

Before Jacob could give his perspective, Lilly shrugged. "It went fine. We filled out some paperwork and answered some questions. I start tomorrow."

His *daed*'s smile dimmed. "Well, how was your teacher?"

"Fine."

The smile completely vanished. "That tells me nothing, Lilly."

"I know, but that's because there wasn't much to tell. It was just school, Dawdi."

"Just school? You used to love school."

"I used to be a lot younger, too."

His *daed* folded his arms across his chest and pretended to look put out. "Lilly Yoder, you start talking this minute. Fill me in."

Hearing his father's gruff voice made Jacob feel like grinning.

Both the tone and the words were classic traits of his busy, inquisitive father. He liked to talk, ask questions, and listen to answers. He also was bossy, but all bark and no bite. People who didn't know him were a bit afraid of him, but not his children. Or his grandchildren. Lilly—who was usually shy and reserved with most people—became just as bossy whenever she was around him.

Still, though Jacob knew his father's questions and mannerisms were based in love, he feared that his niece might not feel that way. She had recently lost her parents and been relocated to Charm. For her grandfather to demand answers about something she didn't want to discuss was a mistake.

"Daed, Lilly is right; there really isn't too much to share. All the other kids were gone when we got there."

"That's too bad. Well, tomorrow will surely be a great day. A wonderful-*gut* one."

Lilly shook her head. "Not really, Dawdi. I won't know anyone. All my friends are back in Berlin."

"I'm sure in no time you will have made some good friends here, too," Jacob said. "At least your teacher seems nice."

"I suppose." Lilly shifted from one foot to the other. It was obvious she couldn't wait to escape their company. "I'm going to go to my room now."

"Not so fast," Daed ordered.

Jacob inhaled, ready to intervene if his father pushed much harder—or if Lilly's withdrawn manner veered toward rude. "You're all grown-up now, but I haven't seen you all day. Give your poor old grandfather a quick hug before you disappear."

"You ain't old, Dawdi," she said as she gave him a quick hug—and her first real smile since walking in. "You're perfect."

"I feel old today," he said gruffly. "All right then. Go say hello to your *mommi* before you go hide in your room. She made you cookies."

After she walked to the kitchen, Daed looked at Jacob. "Sounds like today was tough on Lilly."

Jacob nodded. "I think it was. I don't know why she's not excited about school anymore. She used to love going, but today she looked like she wished she was anywhere else."

"She's probably missing her old friends."

"Maybe, or maybe not. It didn't feel as if she was only missing friends." Thinking back to Lilly's behavior, he said, "It seemed like she didn't really care about school. Maybe something happened at her old one?"

"Who knows?" Daed frowned. "If something did, Marc and Anne never told me."

Yet again, Jacob wished he'd stayed in better contact with his older brother. They hadn't had discussions about anything of worth in years. Then, just two months ago, Marc and Anne had died suddenly in an accident. That had set off a chain of events everyone was still trying to come to terms with. Now, here was Jacob, trying to parent a thirteen-year-old girl whom he'd not only never spent much time with, but had never really gotten to know.

After darting a quick look toward the kitchen, Daed said, "Tell me about the teacher. Who is at the school now?"

"Rachel Mast. Do you know her?"

"*Nee*. Well, what was she like? Did she seem nice?"

Thinking about Rachel's sweet personality and white-blond hair, Jacob blurted, "She seemed kind. Young, too. Probably no more than twenty or twenty-one years old. She's married already."

Daed smiled. "Sounds like she was snapped up. I married your *mamm* at eighteen."

Jacob didn't even want to go down that road. If he did, his father would take care to remind him that he was twenty-eight. At least once a week, his parents reminded him that it was time to take a wife. Past time. "Anyway, Rachel had a friend who was there volunteering."

"Oh? And who was that?"

"Rebecca Kinsinger," he said with a smile. She was a fetching thing, so earnest and wholesome looking, with a tad amount of mischief in her eyes. And that dimple. He never thought he'd be the type of man to notice such things, but he had hardly been able to look away.

His father grinned. "Now, I do know Rebecca. She's always been a pretty girl. Not as pretty as her sister, of course, but she's always had a way about her that I've found appealing."

Jacob had thought she was mighty appealing, too. "I thought she was real pretty. And nice."

"I hope she is nice. After all, my granddaughter needs as many caring people in her life as possible right now."

Forcing his thoughts back on Lilly, Jacob nodded. "I agree. To be honest, I'm a little worried about her. Lilly hardly said five words to me the whole way here."

"She'll come around." After a moment, he cocked his head and smiled. "Don't you hear her chatting with your mother? Lilly just needs time and care."

Jacob crossed his arms over his chest. "I don't know how you do it, Daed, but you make parenting look so easy."

As he always did whenever Jacob gave him a compliment, his father flushed with pleasure while brushing off his words. "Parenting is easy, Jacob. All you have to do is listen, be available, and remain positive."

Jacob was learning that his father's simple advice was easier said than done. So far, raising a thirteen-year-old was proving to be anything but easy.

After Marc and Anne's deaths, Jacob had known he needed to do something. His parents were too old to care for a thirteen-year-old girl. At least, that had been Jacob and his sister Mary's opinions. Mary had six children of her own with her husband, Bill, and she worried that suddenly being around loud children all the time might be too much for Lilly. She was, after all, an only child.

After talking about it with Mary, Jacob made the decision to move from Pinecraft, Florida, to Charm, Ohio, to help with his parents' farm and become Lilly's new guardian. But he soon discovered that good intentions and grand ideas didn't always lend themselves to successful enterprises. Lilly was still mourning her parents' deaths, and moving to a new place wasn't easy.

His parents had given Lilly time to settle into her new room at the farm. She'd been so down about starting at the new school, they'd let her sit out the first few days before enrolling her. But none of those activities had seemed to lift the girl's spirits.

"I'm trying to be positive, but it's hard. Most of the time Lilly barely listens to me. I wish she'd try to meet me halfway sometimes." Of course, the moment those words left his mouth, he regretted them. "Forget I said that. I didn't mean to sound so uncaring, Daed. I know Lilly is struggling. I'll get better and learn to be more patient with her."

His father brushed off his apology with a wave of his hand.

"Don't apologize. You didn't say anything wrong. You are simply being honest."

There was honesty, and then there was being a little too harsh with a young girl who had lost so much. "I shouldn't even be thinking things like that. I know better."

"Jake. Stop fretting so much. You're right, the girl has a heap on her plate, but she will bear it. The Lord will make sure of it."

"Yes. Of course."

"It's only been two months. Grief takes time. Always does."

When he said things like that, it reminded Jacob of just how much he'd missed his parents. He'd missed their wisdom and kindness, and especially the way they easily put everything into perspective. "I know you are right."

"*Nee*, we hope and pray I am right. The Lord will help and guide us . . . if we remember to give Him a chance, *jah?*"

"*Jah*. I hope and pray Lilly will adjust to her new life soon."

But instead of receiving more encouragement, this time, his father merely slapped him on the back with a gruff laugh. "Listen to you, son. You are sounding more and more like a father with each passing day. One day our Lilly will realize how much you care about her. Don't despair; she doesn't have to like you all the time, she just has to know that you love her."

"I do love her." In spite of his doubt about ever being the father his brother was, Jacob smiled. "I've told her that, too. So, that's *gut*, right?"

"It is good, indeed. Wonderful-*gut*. As long as that girl knows she's loved, anything can be overcome."

Though the words were beautiful, Jacob wondered if they were a bit too simplistic. Lilly had lost both of her parents, been forced to change schools for her final year, and now had only her uncle and a pair of elderly grandparents to rely on. Any one of those things would be hard enough for her to bear. Combined? It would give even the most well-adjusted teenager a difficult time.

However, he wasn't about to say a word about that. "*Danke*, Daed. Those are wise words."

"Of course they are. I'm a wise man," he said with a wink before shuffling off to the kitchen.

Standing alone in the foyer, Jacob grinned. His father was a wise man, but, it seemed, he was also quite full of himself. He hadn't changed much, if at all. Jacob realized suddenly that he wouldn't want it any other way.

It was good to be home.

# Chapter 3

*That same day*

A lone at last.

After closing the schoolhouse door, Rachel Mast walked back down the row of desks, running a hand along the surface of the wood as she did so. All in all, everything was fairly neat and organized. She already had her lesson plans for the next day neatly written out. All she had to do was record some grades and write the morning activity on the chalkboard. If she hurried, she could grab her tote and purse and start her walk home within the next twenty minutes.

But she wasn't in a hurry.

Instead, she walked to the gliding rocker in the corner of the room, sat, and leaned back with a smile. At last, she could finally let Agnes's words settle into her heart. She was going to have a baby.

Rachel had been almost certain that was the case, but today's appointment with the midwife had confirmed it. In a little less than nine months, she and Marcus were going to have their own family.

Thinking about her husband, she sighed with happiness. Marcus was going to be so happy. Overjoyed.

Though they'd only been married a little more than a year, he'd been open about how much he hoped they'd start their family soon. This wasn't a surprise. He was ten years older than she was. He'd been courting her ever since her father had given him permission when she was seventeen. It had been a slow courtship, too. For months, she spent only a few hours with him every week. Though she'd been flattered by his attention, she hadn't been sure that she'd wanted a husband who was so much older than she.

But over three years, he'd proven himself to be everything she ever wanted. He was easy to talk to, handsome and strong, and had a good job. A really good one—he was a team leader over at Kinsinger's Lumber. He'd also been supportive with her dreams. She'd always wanted to be a schoolteacher. When the position at Charm Amish School opened up, Rachel had jumped at it.

She'd soon discovered that the job was everything she'd ever hoped it would be. She loved her students and loved being with them all day. But now it seemed that things were changing again.

Hopefully, Rebecca Kinsinger would eventually settle in to the swing of things and be able to take over the class when the baby came. Then? Well, Rachel supposed her future was up to the Lord.

She was pretty sure that her teaching days were almost over, though.

Rocking back and forth, Rachel sighed. As much as she wanted a baby and to make Marcus happy, she was going to miss this place. Her mother had always assured her that the Lord gave each person special gifts. Her mother's gifts were in her quilting. She not only designed and made beautiful quilts for their family and friends, but she also made several a year to sell in order to help the family's finances. Daed always said Mamm's nimble fingers were responsible for their comfortable savings account. Because of her, they'd never had to worry about illnesses or their future.

From the time she was five or six, Rachel had known her gifts revolved around teaching children. She'd taught her little brother and sisters, even her dolls and stuffed teddy bear. She'd practically had tears in her eyes on her first day of school, she'd been so excited.

But now that she was going to have a child of her own, she was going to have to give up her time in this classroom. Of course she looking forward to the opportunity to teach her own *kinner*. But it wasn't going to be the same.

"Wishes and dreams are for children. Shame on you, Rachel, for thinking about anything negative on such a special day." It was time to go home and tell her husband the happy news.

She'd just gathered her things together when the door burst open.

Her heart hammering in her chest, she gasped, then laughed at her husband's panicked expression. "Marcus Mast, what are you doing here?"

Striding forward, he reached for her hands. "The question should be why are *you* still here? And what were you doing today at Agnes's *haus*?"

"I'm still here because I had to put this room to rights. You know how I like to spend time in here after all the children go home." With a bit of trepidation, she said, "How did you know I saw Agnes?"

"One of the men at work mentioned that he saw you enter her *haus*." He frowned. "Are you ill? And if you are, why didn't you tell me?" Before she could reply, he reached for her hand. "Besides, you know how I feel about Agnes. She's old and crotchety. If you aren't well, you need to go to the clinic, not to that old woman."

Squeezing his hands, she smiled. "Which question would you like me to answer first?"

"Don't tease me, Rachel." His dark eyes scanned her face. "You don't know what I've been going through. I had to wait to get over here until we finished completing our order of trusses for that home builder in Michigan. It took forever." Exhaling, he said, "What is going on?"

Well, this certainly wasn't the way she'd hoped to tell him about their babe. But ever since the accident at the mill, her sweet husband seemed to be on edge. He liked to know where she was at every moment of the day. "I'm pregnant," she said simply.

His expression went blank. "Already?"

Taking care not to look amused at his shocked expression, she nodded and squeezed his hand again. "I thought it might be the case, but I didn't want to get your hopes up until I was sure."

"Ah."

Her amusement at his confusion faded and was replaced by concern. "This isn't how I thought you'd react. Aren't you happy?"

"*Jah*. I mean, yes. Yes, of course." He took off his hat, closed his eyes, and rubbed a hand over his face. "I'm just surprised. It took my *mamm* years to have a child. I had assumed that would be the case for us, too."

Letting go of his hand, she stepped closer so she could lean in for a hug. When he exhaled, she leaned close, enjoying how strong and solid he felt. "You know my mother had five children in seven years. Sometimes these things don't take too long."

"I guess not." With obvious care, he wrapped his arms around her and cuddled her close. At last. "*Danke*, Rachel. You made me mighty happy. Before you know it, I'll be rushing off work to get home to you and our babe, and this classroom will be a thing of the past."

His words pinched. But instead of going down that path, she pressed her face into his neck and breathed in his familiar, clean scent. He was a good man. The best. He cared for her deeply and he always had. She had just made him happy. That was what mattered—not that she was going to have to give up her dream of being a teacher far too soon.

She needed to remember that.

REBECCA GOT HOME just in time for supper. After washing up, she helped Darla and Amelia place the country-fried steak, mashed potatoes, thick cream gravy, and roasted carrots on the table.

A few months ago, she had apologized for not helping to prepare the meals. But when she'd seen the flash of hurt in Amelia's eyes, Rebecca had realized that she needed to simply be appreciative of Amelia's efforts. After all, her sister was an excellent cook and an even better homemaker. She didn't need help cooking their meals. Now, Rebecca simply made sure that she complimented her sister on a fine meal.

Having Darla in the house was a welcome change, too. When she married Lukas, Lukas had offered to move to her family's home so she could continue to help care for her siblings.

But Darla's oldest siblings, Aaron and Patsy, had firmly pushed aside that idea. After depending on Darla to do so much, they were happy to take over the running of the family. Darla had accepted their wishes without argument. Rebecca thought she was grateful to have some time to concentrate on herself and her new husband.

Darla's presence also seemed to ease Lukas's worries about Levi's absence. And her large family helped, too. Whether it was because of Amelia's talents in the kitchen or because Darla was missed, usually one or two of Darla's siblings joined them each day for the evening meal. Rebecca enjoyed the novelty of having guests for supper. Each one of Darla's six siblings added something different to the conversation. It was also heartwarming to see how much Darla enjoyed their company.

Tonight, it was Evan, one of Darla's younger twin brothers, who stopped by. He was fourteen and had a good sense of humor. After Rebecca, Amelia, and Darla joined Evan and Lukas at the table, the five of them bowed their heads in silent prayer.

Then the chaos began.

It had always been like this. When they were little and both of their parents had been alive, whoever was present at dinner seemed to transform once they sat at their old, sturdy oak table. Suddenly everyone had an opinion about everything and had a need to voice it, loudly and proudly. If someone disagreed, they were ignored or talked over.

Usually Rebecca enjoyed the conversations. They were lively and fun and often a bit humorous, but never without laughter.

Tonight's conversation centered on something near and dear to her heart—her bulldog puppy, Oscar.

"My Oscar is a *gut hund*," she said. "The best." Looking down at him, she thought again how handsome he was, with his white coat and brown spots and ears. She'd always thought he looked as if he'd gotten mixed up in a bucket of white paint.

"Not hardly," her normally sweet-natured sister countered. "Your puppy ate my *kapp*."

Rebecca couldn't help but point out the obvious. "Since it's on your head, I don't think you're much worse for wear."

"This is my second-best *kapp*. My best one, the one I just bought at Miller's, is shredded to pieces. Your dog had a mighty fun time destroying it, too."

"I doubt he enjoyed it. He didn't know what he was doing. He's just a puppy. And remember, puppies chew."

"I am sorry to say this, Rebecca," Darla commented, "but I think I must side with Amelia. I saw Oscar running around the house with its remains. The *kapp*'s ties were hanging out of his mouth. He looked right proud of himself."

"He lumbered," Lukas corrected. "I don't think that chubby dog is capable of running."

"He's not chubby. It's how he is made."

"He's cute, for sure," Evan said.

"*Danke*, Evan. You may come over for supper tomorrow night, too."

While Rebecca grinned at the boy, Darla tilted her head as if she was actually trying to weigh Lukas's words. "*Lumbering* is a good description, I think."

Amelia scowled. "Whatever he did, my *kapp* is ruined."

"Honestly, Amelia, it's not the end of the world."

One perfectly arched eyebrow lifted. "It's the end of that *kapp*."

"Fine. I'll buy you a new one."

"*Danke.*"

Considering how easily her little sister accepted that, Rebecca suspected that had been her goal all along. "But, just for the record, I think you need to start putting your things out of his reach. Or maybe close your bedroom door."

"Really, Rebecca?" Amelia said, a look of irritation playing over her usually composed features.

Lukas groaned. "Let's not start this. I canna take another argument about nothing."

Amelia jutted out her chin. "Just because this doesn't concern you, it don't mean it's nothing, *bruder*."

"Don't twist my words, sister."

Darla placed a steadying hand on Lukas's arm then turned to Evan with a bright smile. It was obviously pasted on, but Rebecca was impressed with her effort.

"Evan, how was seeing your sister-in-law at school today?"

And just like that, all thoughts about Oscar and shredded *kapps* ceased to be important. Bracing herself to hear the boy's criticism, Rebecca set her fork down and waited. She knew she hadn't done a good job filling in for Rachel.

After looking at her warily, Evan averted his eyes. "Oh, I don't know."

"What does that mean? I'm sure it was a nice change to have Rebecca there."

Evan moved a couple of beans around on his plate before replying. "Um, well, we all really like Miss Rachel. She's a *gut* teacher." Looking a bit apologetic, he added, "We're real used to her ways, too."

Rebecca felt her face heat. There it was. A teenaged boy carefully sidestepping her inadequacies, right there for everyone to see. Not wanting to meet Evan's eyes, she speared a couple of beans on her fork, too.

After helping himself to another heaping spoonful of mashed potatoes, Lukas looked her way. "What did you do, Rebecca?"

"Nothing."

"Really?"

"Well, I was only in charge for an hour."

"Was that all? It seemed a lot longer than that," Evan said.

Of course, it had felt that way, too. Rebecca caught Amelia's eyes widening before she carefully hid her expression.

Something about seeing that even her little sister knew she was a hopeless teacher was a rather bitter pill to swallow. "I was there longer, but I didn't do too much while Rachel was in charge." Rebecca felt her cheeks flush. "If you want to know the truth, I soon learned that looking after twenty-five *kinner* is harder than it looks."

Lukas rolled his eyes. "How can it be so hard? They're just children."

"Trust me. Children are not easy to handle. Some of them, like that Peter Schlabach, are right difficult."

"He was only difficult because you called him a child, Rebecca," Evan said. "All the kids made fun of him on the way home."

"I didn't mean anything by it." She sighed. "But *jah*. I figured that out really fast, too. Still, he should have acted better."

"He always acts good when he's at work," Lukas pointed out. "He's one of the hardest-working teenagers we've ever had. We're going to let him deliver mail soon."

Rebecca shrugged. "I don't know what happened, exactly. All I know is that if Rachel hadn't come in when she did, that boy's behavior would have gotten even worse."

Lukas frowned. "Want me to talk to him?"

"Of course not. If you say anything, he's going to think I tattled."

"You kind of did," Amelia pointed out.

Rebecca rolled her eyes. "You tattled on Oscar."

"That *hund* ate my *kapp*."

"Maybe your next visit will go better," Darla said encouragingly.

"Maybe, though it might not." Actually, she was thinking she had quite a ways to go before she could consider her time in the classroom a success.

"Maybe you should stick to working at the mill," Lukas said. "I don't want to ruin your dream of being a teacher, but we really missed you there. You're a mighty *gut* receptionist."

"Lukas, you shouldn't have said that," Darla chided.

"Why not? It's true. She's wonderful-*gut*."

"That might be so, but everyone needs to follow their heart."

Right before their eyes, her bossy brother softened. "That is true," he said with a smile. "Look what happened to us."

"Oh, no," Evan grumbled. "You two aren't going to start fawning over each other again, are you?"

"Evan, you are a guest here," Darla said. "Mind your manners."

"I'm also your *bruder*. And I don't want to watch you get all mushy over your husband." Then, as if he suddenly realized who that husband was, he flushed. "Sorry, Lukas."

"I don't blame you. If Levi was here, he would have said something far more direct."

The mention of Levi put an immediate damper on the conversation.

"I hope Levi is okay," Amelia whispered. "I wish he'd come home."

Their supper conversation tonight was a veritable minefield of taboo topics. Grasping for another subject to raise their spirits, Rebecca said, "Guess what, Evan? I did meet a new student this afternoon."

"Oh? Boy or girl?"

"Girl, and her name is Lilly. She is thirteen. She's going to start tomorrow."

"Where's she from?"

"I'm not sure. I thought her *daed* said he was from Florida, but the girl said something about how she was from Ohio. Anyway, she seemed really nice."

"We'll see." Evan shrugged. "Girls her age aren't always so nice to boys."

"You're a full year older than her, Evan," Darla said.

"*Jah*. But to some girls, that don't matter one bit."

The silly, sweet comment was so true and irreverent, Rebecca giggled. And just like that, all of her problems faded away. Lukas chuckled, Darla shook her head in dismay, and Amelia grinned down at her plate.

As Rebecca smiled at Evan, she gave thanks for him. His simple statement was a nice reminder that everything mattered to someone. No matter how big or small it might seem, it was still important.

# Chapter 4

*Monday, August 17*

Four days later, Rebecca wished she could return to the wonderful feeling of contentment that she'd felt at her supper table. Instead, she was once again sitting behind the circular reception desk of Kinsinger Lumber. The broad granite countertops that surrounded her were covered with piles of folders she hadn't sorted and messages she'd neither had time to read nor reply to. Phones had been incessantly ringing, customers in the retail showroom had been asking questions, and deliverymen from no less than three companies had stopped to ask her for help.

She was also currently surrounded by a handful of men, each of whom was acting as if his business was more important than the others.

"One at a time, please," she bit out. Again. When they quieted, she turned to the man who'd been standing there the longest. "Now, Jonas, what invoice did you say you had concerns about?"

"The invoice marked July seventh. I told you that," he said impatiently.

She ignored the jab and wrote down his reminder. "I'll look into it." Turning to the next man, she said, "Scott, tell me what it was that you needed again."

"I need you to call Griffin Mill in Washington State."

She wrote that down. "Because?"

"Their latest shipment of redwood is running two weeks late. The customers who ordered it want some answers. But no one at Griffin is answering my calls."

Though Rebecca wasn't sure why Scott thought anyone would pick up her calls if they weren't picking up his, she still wrote down his concerns dutifully. "I'll call this afternoon."

"*Danke.*" He leaned closer. "And, Becky, when you get an answer, don't forget to let me know as soon as possible."

Rebecca nodded, keeping her thoughts to herself about how she definitely did not have time to trot down to Scott's building to give him updates. "Next?" she asked wearily.

Abe smacked his palm down on her desk as if he didn't already have her full attention. "I need to put in for some vacation, Rebecca."

Her patience nearing its end, she shook her head. "You know you should go to your team leader. I canna take care of vacation leave for a whole company."

"I know that," Abe replied, looking just as irritated to be talking to her as she was to be hearing about vacation leave. "However, my team leader is Jeremy Wolfe. He's out sick. I was told that you were his backup."

Shoving a notecard his way, she said, "Write all the pertinent details down, and I'll take care of it. Next?"

"We need to check on our fundraiser," Paul said. "It's sched-uled to take place in six weeks but I don't think anything's get-ting organized."

Pulling her spiral notebook closer, Rebecca scribbled *Fund-raiser. Paul. Check.* Hopefully when she finally got to that note she'd remember what it meant, though it was doubtful.

And so it continued. Four more workers, plus one retail cus-tomer, and one builder representative, all with questions and de-mands. An hour later, after assuring everyone that she could get to his needs far more quickly if he was not watching her every move, Rebecca shooed them all away. Each person left grudg-ingly.

"You're sure you won't forget about Griffin Mill?" Scott asked.

"I will not forget, Scott."

Glad to have a few minutes of peace and quiet, Rebecca rested her head on the back of her chair and sighed. She wasn't sure how much longer she was going to be able to do this full-time.

The men, while always respectful, were men. They were gruff and abrupt. They got sweaty and stomped around. They joked with one another but not with her. She was not only a member of the Kinsinger family, but she was also a woman. Those two factors were always going to keep an imaginary barrier between her and the rest of the workers.

When Rebecca had first started at the reception desk, she'd been a little hurt by the men's distance. Luckily, she'd grown ac-customed to it over the past three years.

She'd tried to find satisfaction in helping her family. And she had. She also got along with most of Lukas's and Levi's friends. They might not ask her to eat lunch with them, but they were friendly enough.

Even so, she was more than a little tired of being in the company of men all day. She was growing weary of every conversation being about lumber and trucks and deliveries and shipments.

Though she appreciated how hard the men in the company worked—and understood their concerns—she was starting to realize that in her heart, she didn't care all that much about what they wanted. The fact was, Rebecca did not want to work at the lumber mill six days a week. She wanted this to be her brothers' place of work. Not hers.

She needed to do something else. She needed it as much as Scott needed his questions answered from Griffin Mill.

When she opened her eyes, she was startled to see Lukas leaning up against the doorframe of his office. His arms were folded over his chest and he was looking at her so intently she thought he was attempting to read her mind.

"How long have you been standing there?" she asked.

Her brother cocked his head to one side. "Long enough to see that you have a to-do list a mile long."

"*Jah*. That about sums it up." She rolled her eyes. "I swear, half of these men don't need a receptionist, they need a mother. They're helpless, Luke."

Though he didn't crack a smile, his gaze warmed. "*Nee*, they simply know who to look to for help. You are a capable woman. I promise, they wouldn't flock around you if they didn't believe you could get things done."

"That's good to know." At the moment, though, she wished she was just a little less competent. Maybe then more people would attempt to solve their own problems instead of asking her to fix them.

Walking toward her, new concern lit his expression. "Hey,

what's going on? You usually don't let any of this get to you. I've seen you handle dozens of moments like the one I just witnessed. Is everything okay?"

"Everything is fine." And it was. Well, as fine as it could be. "I'm sorry. I'm just a little grumpy. I'll get over it."

"You don't have to apologize to me. I know these men and this job can be a handful. I remember Daed made me take over your chair a few months after I started here. He told me I needed to remember how important each person's role in the company was."

She chuckled. "I had forgotten all about that. You hated sitting in this chair."

"*Jah*. I really hated it. I wasn't good at it, either." Rubbing the back of his neck, he said, "I think half the men marched into Daed's office and threatened to quit if he didn't get me out of there."

Rebecca knew he was trying to make her feel better, she really did. But so far all his story was doing was making her wish that she'd gotten to move on, too. "Like I said, I'm fine. I won't feel so overwhelmed once I get some things on my to-do list taken care of."

Lukas didn't look as if he believed her. "You know what, we've been blessed with a lot of work. But because of that, there are lots of minor emergencies. It's stressful. Maybe you need some help."

The last thing in the world she wanted to do was make Lukas more stressed about the mill than he already was. She had no right to complain when he was running a whole business single-handedly. "No worries, I feel much better now. I, um, just needed to vent."

But instead of looking relieved, he sat down in the chair

across from her. "Becky, be honest. What's going on?" After a pause, he looked at her worriedly. "Hey, none of the men are being disrespectful, are they? If someone is treating you poorly, I'll put a stop to that."

"No one is being disrespectful." She quickly shook her head.

"Sure?"

"Positive."

"Okay, then what can we do to make you happier? How about we hire you an assistant? Like I said, the business has been growing. I've hired more managers but not more office assistants."

She loved how Lukas always talked to her as an equal. He valued her abilities to handle things. Because of that, she shrugged. "An assistant might help. I don't know, Luke. Maybe all these changes have finally gotten the best of me."

"If so, we need to ease your load."

She thought about that. "You're right, there is a lot of work to be done, but I don't mind all that much. It's just—" She stopped herself before complaining more. She wasn't a whiner, she never had been. She had always prided herself on simply putting her head down and working harder when things got tough.

"Come on, Becky. Talk to me. I'm not your boss, I'm your brother."

"All right." Unable to stay sitting behind that desk piled high with work, she got up and walked around, leaning against the front of it.

Then, without the desk between herself and her brother, she bared her soul. "It's like this. I think everything has just finally gotten to me. Daed dying, then dealing with the aftermath of the fire. Then you and Darla getting married and Levi leaving. . . . It's kind of a lot to take in."

"It has been a lot. Too much."

"I'll handle it, though."

He looked troubled. "I didn't think you minded that me and Darla got married right away."

"I didn't and I don't. You two are perfect for each other, and you always have been," she said in a rush. "I promise, I'm happy for you. I love Darla. But it's simply another change in an already eventful two years. It's exhausting, trying to keep up."

"It would have been better if Levi hadn't taken off." With a pained expression, he added, "I can't tell you the number of times I've had to reassure Darla that his leaving was not her fault."

Rebecca thought about that. Although Lukas had worried that it was his marriage to Darla that had made Levi so upset, she didn't think that was the reason Levi had left.

She was starting to think that Levi's excuse had been completely honest. All the changes had simply gotten the best of him, too. But instead of staying and working things out, he had opted to take some time for himself.

Though she hated the extra work caused by his leaving, she couldn't say she blamed him. She wanted some time for herself, too.

"Levi leaving was not Darla's fault. I think he would be mighty upset if he knew she thought that."

"He's not going to know, though, because he hasn't kept in touch," Lukas said bitterly. "I can't believe he just took off with nothing more than a brief note saying good-bye."

Rebecca completely agreed. Levi's departure had been painful. Lukas had felt guilty, and she had been perplexed. But Amelia? Amelia had been crushed. They'd always been close, and Amelia took his leaving very personally.

"I think it was simply the last straw."

"I can't do anything about Levi. But I can help you."

"Lukas, please stop worrying so much. I am fine."

Narrowing his eyes, he shook his head. "No, I don't think so."

"Lukas—"

"Rebecca, how about this? How about I ask one of the women who works in the retail store to come work in here with you?"

"Such as?"

He thought for a moment. "How about Mercy? She's awfully good at managing both numbers and people."

Though Rebecca had been prepared to push aside any of his suggestions, that name drew her up short. Mercy was eighteen, smart as a whip, and as brash as a mockingbird. In a strange way, Mercy's youth helped her more than another person's experience might. Pretty much because she had no expectations or fear of failure. Instead of worrying about what might happen if she was disappointed, Mercy merely ran over everyone's objections until she got her way. That pushiness was not a very good quality when making friends but it was excellent when sitting at the reception desk and dealing with all those men day after day.

In a rare show of patience, Lukas let her consider his choice. "Well?" he asked.

"You know what? I think Mercy would do great here." She could actually feel her entire being lighten at the prospect of sharing some of her duties. "I wouldn't have thought of her at first, but I think she would be a good fit."

Lukas grinned. "I think so, too."

"Do you think she'll say yes?" Now that he'd mentioned the idea, she was already hoping it wouldn't go away.

Lukas nodded. "I am sure she will. She doesn't always get

along with our retail customers but she gets along real well with our employees. I can promise you that Scott won't be coming in here any longer and browbeating the receptionist to do his bidding."

Rebecca giggled. "The first time he tries that with Mercy, she's going to bite his head off."

Lukas grinned. "Just like a Doberman." Taking a breath, he turned serious again. "Rebecca, you know how much I like you here. You do a good job, but it's more than that, too."

She suddenly felt shy. "What is it?"

"When I walk out of Daed's old office and see you here, I realize that it's still our family's company. Seeing you here helps me remember that I'm not alone."

"You're not alone, Luke. You've got more support here than you realize. Everyone is real proud of you."

He shrugged. "Everyone just wants things to go on like they used to. I'm doing my best with that."

"You're doing more than that." What her brother didn't realize was that he was so capable and respected, no one would ever suggest that he didn't have every right to run the company. The fact of the matter was that Lukas Kinsinger had always been Kinsinger Lumber. More so than her or Levi.

By making him their parents' eldest son, God had created a perfect match. Lukas not only wanted to take over their family's business, but he was also meant to do so. It hadn't just been their parents who'd been proud of how easily he'd followed in his their father's footsteps; they had all been proud of him.

"I'm glad I can help you, Lukas. I like feeling needed, and I like having a connection to our family's business. I don't ever want to give up being here completely, but I don't think that working behind this desk is the future that the Lord intends for me."

"I can understand you wanting to follow the Lord's will. But, not to be mean . . . are you sure He wants you to be a teacher?"

She smiled at him so he would know that she wasn't offended. "I don't know if He wants me to be a teacher or not. Right now, I know I'm not too great at it. However, I do know that I like being around the kids. I like helping them. Right now I like helping Rachel. And even though I'm not trained to be a teacher and I'm making lots of mistakes, I like it, Lukas. I truly do."

Understanding filled his expression. "Liking a job counts for a lot, I think."

"*Jah*. I think so, too. The hours I've spent at school helping her have made me feel energized, not exhausted. I go home smiling instead of irritated."

He nodded. "I'll go talk to Mercy now. If she's agreeable to the new job, I'll send her up here. How about you train her for the rest of the week, then move to part time?"

"You would let me do that?" Although she was admittedly ready for a change, she'd never expected it would happen so quickly.

"I want you happy, Becky. Your happiness means a lot to me."

"I want you happy, too. I don't want to give you more stress than you're already feeling."

"I'll be happy if I know that you're happy. And I can't deny that I'm looking forward to watching Mercy run roughshod over some of our more bossy employees."

She laughed. "I'm almost going to feel sorry for them. Almost."

"Just remember that if you change your mind, you can always go back to full time."

"*Danke*, Luke."

Looking completely sincere, he added, "But more importantly, you will always mean the world to me. No matter what happens with work or Darla or whomever you end up with. We'll always have each other."

"*Jah*. That's what's most important, Luke. Family is always most important."

"Some days, it's all we have."

Those words couldn't have been more true.

# Chapter 5

*Tuesday, August 18*

The algebraic equation was giving Lilly fits. No matter how many times she went over it, she couldn't figure out what to do with the missing variable. Eyeing the equation she'd copied down from the textbook she'd found at the library, she realized she was going to need to erase the figures she'd written and work through the whole thing again. One way or another, she was going to figure this out. She had to, so she could get to the harder problems she'd discovered in the back of the book.

After making sure that Mrs. Mast was still occupied with a group of little kids at the front of the classroom, Lilly pulled out her eraser and got to work.

"What are you doing?" Katie asked.

"Nothing."

Ignoring her comment, her new friend leaned closer and peered at Lilly's paper. "That ain't our homework."

"I know." She covered it up with her palm. "It's nothing. I was just playing around."

Katie wrinkled her nose. "With a bunch of numbers and letters? You sure have a strange idea of fun."

Embarrassed that she was doing algebra for fun, Lilly tried to laugh off her friend's statement. "I know. I was just bored. Like I said, it wasn't anything. What's going on with you?"

Katie blushed. "Nothing."

Lilly noticed that Katie didn't have her homework out on her desk. "You better get your papers out. When Mrs. Mast gets done meeting with the little kids, she's going to come this way and start collecting our work."

"I don't have it done."

"Why not?"

"My *daed* put up a tire swing last night over our pond. Me and my brothers swung on it all evening. I was planning to do it after I got in bed but I fell asleep."

Lilly had never not done her homework. However, she knew better than to say anything about that. Katie was like a lot of girls their age. When they got to be thirteen, they started caring less about school and more about what they'd be doing when they graduated.

Because of that, Lilly concentrated on Katie's story. "Why did your *daed* put the swing over the pond?"

"So we could swing over the water and jump in, of course." Her eyes glowed. "It's so fun."

"I bet." It took some effort, but Lilly did her best to sound interested and not jealous. Katie had no idea how blessed she was to have parents and siblings. She only had grandparents and an uncle who couldn't farm worth beans.

Of course, the moment that thought ran through her head, she felt guilty. From the moment she'd arrived in Charm, her grandparents and uncle had bent over backward to make her feel at home. They'd held her when she'd cried and talked about her *mamm* and *daed* for hours whenever she wanted. They'd also allowed her to have the space she needed to adjust.

Katie was all smiles now. "Have you ever done that?"

"Hmm?"

"Swung into the water. Have you done it?"

"*Nee.*" It sounded scary.

"You should come over one day and go swimming." Looking concerned, she said, "You can swim, right?"

"I can swim." Not very well, but she could float. And she could hold her breath under the water. She had a feeling that wasn't near good enough to jump from a swing into deep water, however.

Katie looked relieved. "I'm only teasing ya. My parents said you came from Florida. I bet everyone practically grows up in the water there."

"All of Florida isn't next to water, you know."

"I know that. But—"

"And that was my uncle who came from Florida. I'm from Berlin."

"Oh, *jah*. Because your parents died."

Unable to respond to that, Lilly nodded and stared back at her paper.

Peter Schlabach, who so far hadn't said all that much to her, scowled at Katie. "Wow, Kate. You sure know how to pick the wrong thing to say."

After peeking to make sure Mrs. Mast still wasn't nearby,

Katie glared at Peter. "Shut up, Peter." Then, before he could volley an angry retort, she turned back to Lilly. "I'm sorry I said anything. I shouldn't have brought up your parents."

While Peter muttered something sarcastic under his breath, Lilly simply nodded. She knew her friend hadn't intended to be mean. She was simply a blunt girl. It wasn't her fault that Lilly felt embarrassed. She hated being different.

After fishing around in her desk, Katie stood up with a sigh. Then she walked to the back of the room to sharpen her pencil.

Lilly was just about to open up that textbook again when Peter slipped into Katie's empty seat.

"Don't pay her any mind," he said quietly.

"It's okay. It's not her fault that I'm so sensitive."

"Sure it is." When she gaped at him, he smirked. "Believe me, Katie always says the wrong thing. She's been that way her whole life. I tell you what, she's really good at it, too."

Even though she knew she shouldn't, Lilly smiled. "*Danke* for that."

"You live off of Route 557, right?"

"*Jah*. At my grandparents' farm."

"I live real close to you." Staring at her intently, he lowered his voice. "Want to walk home together?"

Just as his question sunk in, Lilly noticed Katie returning to her seat and Mrs. Mast eyeing her and Peter curiously.

Lilly wasn't sure why she did it, maybe she was simply trying to get him to move, but she nodded. It surely didn't have anything to do with the fact that his brown eyes were framed by thick black eyelashes or that she felt like he didn't notice anyone else in the world when he stared at her.

He grinned as he walked back to his seat.

When Katie took her chair back, she whispered, "What did Peter want?"

"Nothing."

"Sure?"

*"Jah."*

"Hey, want to help me do my homework?"

By now, Lilly knew "help" meant "do." Darting a wary glance at the teacher, she murmured, "I better not. I don't want to get in trouble."

Since Katie didn't look pleased, Lilly stared at the equation in front of her again. At the moment, that math problem looked a whole lot easier to solve than trying to figure out what she thought about Peter asking to walk her home.

Deciding at last to isolate the variable and then multiply, she pulled out her sharpest pencil and got to work.

Around her, kids talked and laughed. They shuffled their papers and complained about homework.

She concentrated on X and Y. Not Peter's offer. Not Katie's questions. Not the fact that she didn't have a *daed* to make tire swings.

"Lilly, what are you working on?" Mrs. Mast asked by her side.

Drat! She hadn't even realized their teacher had gotten so close. "Nothing." Too slowly, she covered the equation.

Mrs. Mast pulled the paper off her desk and studied it. After a few seconds, she blinked, then frowned at it. "Where did you see this?"

"In a textbook."

"Where? We don't have anything like that here."

Fearing she was drawing attention, Lilly lowered her voice. "The library."

After studying the paper again, Mrs. Mast crouched down by her side. "Do you understand this?"

"Kind of."

"Do you know what kind of math you're doing?"

Lilly noticed that her teacher wasn't frowning. Instead, she was smiling in an encouraging way. It made her feel brave. "Algebra?"

"*Jah*, you are," Mrs. Mast said softly. "Did you, um, study algebra at your old school?"

Feeling more than a couple of the other students' attention on her, Lilly shook her head. "*Nee*. I was just interested in it. So I decided to try teaching myself."

"I see."

Lilly pulled out her spiral notebook for math. Flipping it open, she showed it to her teacher. "I did last night's homework. I promise."

Mrs. Mast took the notebook out of her hands. After she scanned it, she set it back down on Lilly's desk. "How long did it take you to do yesterday's math assignment?"

Still feeling like everyone was listening, she shrugged. "I don't know."

"Please be honest with me. You're not in trouble."

"It didn't take me long," she hedged.

"About how long?" Mrs. Mast pressed.

"Ten minutes, maybe?"

"Ten minutes!" Katie exclaimed, her voice high and incredulous. "It would have taken me at least an hour."

Mrs. Mast turned to Katie and frowned. "Would have?"

"I never got it done," Katie admitted.

"It took me longer than that," Peter said. "Hey, Lilly, how come you got done so fast?"

"I don't know," Lilly said, feeling worse than miserable. "I'm *gut* at math."

Mrs. Mast bent down. "We'll talk about this later, okay?"

*"Jah."*

Her teacher squeezed her shoulder before walking over toward a group of girls hunched over some flashcards on the floor.

Once their teacher was out of earshot, Katie leaned close. "Are you showing off?"

*"Nee."*

She frowned. "It sure seemed like it."

"She's not, Katie," Peter interjected. "She's just smart."

"But still—"

"And there's nothing wrong with that," Peter said. "At all," he added a little bit more loudly. His tone was so sure and confident, it was like he was practically daring everyone in the room to argue with him. Then, to Lilly's surprise, he grinned. "Actually, now I know who to go to if I ever need help with math."

Lilly didn't say anything, but inside, she was smiling. She wasn't sure what had just happened, but she was sure it was something big.

Peter Schlabach, who was so cute, so intimidating, and so . . . well, everything, had not only just asked to walk her home but had also told the whole class that he thought it was good that she was really smart.

Just when she'd been sure that things were going from bad to worse . . . they'd gotten pretty good.

Maybe even better than that.

# Chapter 6

R ebecca was impressed. Although Lukas had a whole
company to run, he made it a priority to help her. Soon
after their conversation, he had offered Mercy the job at
the reception desk.

As Lukas had predicted, Mercy had jumped at the chance to
stop serving customers in the retail shop and start bossing workers around. After one day together, Rebecca knew that Mercy
and her new position were a match made in heaven. She was
efficient, she was spunky, and she was cute. She could also trade
barbs and stories with the workers.

After a few days, the men actually started congregating
around the reception area for reasons besides work. Mercy was
bright and full of energy and made everyone laugh. In fact,
rumor had it that the girl was fitting into all the responsibili-
ties of the receptionist desk with the ease of a man slipping on
an old, comfortable shoe. Though Mercy would no doubt find

exception with the analogy, Rebecca couldn't help but feel a bit jealous. It was becoming apparent—to Rebecca, at least—that completely switching occupations was actually easy for some people.

For three days now, she'd been helping out Rachel in her classroom. *Helping*, unfortunately, had been the operative word. Rebecca couldn't seem to juggle all of the students' needs with ease. Just when she was pleased with herself for doing one thing—like memorizing everyone's name—she would mess up in another area.

Yesterday's fiasco had been reading the wrong answers to a science quiz out loud to the older kids. They'd all acted extremely put out with her for not only unnecessarily marking up their papers with red ink, but wasting their time.

Rebecca couldn't blame them. She'd been a good student, regularly earning A's. She had taken her studies and grades seriously, too. If some wayward volunteer had messed up the answer key, she would have made her displeasure known.

While Rachel had seemed pleased to have another pair of helping hands, especially with the little ones, Rebecca was feeling more overwhelmed with each passing hour. The longer she was in the classroom, the more she was coming to understand that she had a lot to learn.

Today had gone better, however. While Rachel worked with the youngest students on their writing, Rebecca had met with the five eldest ones for math. All of her experience in the mill was coming in handy as she showed the girls and boys how to convert metric measurements to inches.

It seemed her experience at the lumber mill made up for some of her inadequacies as a teacher. All of the teenagers enjoyed hearing about what happened at the mill, no doubt because many of their fathers worked there. Rebecca was pleased she could share a number of humorous stories about truckers, shipments, train cargo that arrived, and the Englisher customers who came in from time to time.

Darla's little brothers, Samuel and Evan, also helped by asking her for stories that they knew everyone would like to hear. Plus, they glared at students who looked ready to give their sister-in-law a hard time. Though their support wasn't exactly necessary, Rebecca couldn't help but share her thanks. The past year had taught her never to take kindness for granted.

The only person in her group who didn't look all that excited about her math lesson was Lilly Yoder. Though she wasn't rude or disrespectful, she seemed particularly quiet. Rebecca also caught her scribbling in a worn spiral notebook. Time and again, Lilly would quietly take the worksheet or book assignment Rebecca had given, work on it for a while, and then put it aside and scribble in her notebook again.

To make matters worse, the other girls suddenly seemed not to like Lilly very much. Katie, in particular, went out of her way to ignore her. It looked as if Lilly was being treated the same way as Rebecca—barely tolerated.

The situation bothered Rebecca enough to approach Rachel about it at the end of the day. Unfortunately, Rachel had plans after school and was eager to lock up and go home.

Because of that—and because she couldn't help but continually go over every moment in the classroom and try to figure out how things could have gone better—Rebecca was walking fairly quickly down the narrow path that led from the school yard to the main streets of Charm.

That's when she noticed that Lilly was walking home by herself. She was walking slowly, seeming to be in no hurry. Rebecca felt so sorry for her. She'd recently learned that Lilly's parents had been killed in an accident and that Jacob was actually her uncle. And to make things even harder, she was now the new girl at school.

Rebecca decided to take a chance and walk by her side for a bit.

"Hey, Lilly," she called out when she caught up to her. "Do you mind if I walk with you for a few minutes?"

Lilly blinked at her in surprise, as if she had been lost in thought. "Of course not."

"*Danke*. I'm heading to the mill," Rebecca explained. "Are you heading home now?"

She shook her head. *"Nee."*

"Oh? Where are you off to?"

"The market. I told my *dawdi* that I'd pick him up some apples on my way home from school."

"That's nice of you. I guess it is apple season. My sister Amelia makes the best pies. She's baked a pie for us two Sundays in a row."

"That's nice."

"Are you going to bake a pie?"

"*Nee*. I think my grandmother is." She smiled politely, then stared straight ahead. It was fairly obvious that Lilly wasn't all that excited to be speaking with Rebecca.

But still she persevered. "So, how are things going? Are you settling into school now? Do you like Charm? Are you studying different things than what you were used to in Berlin?"

"Charm is okay. Everything is fine." She looked at Rebecca warily. "Did Mrs. Mast ask you to talk to me about school? Did I do something wrong?"

"Not at all. I, well, I thought maybe we could chat."

"About what?"

"Nothing in particular." When Lilly raised her eyebrows and looked like she was about to walk away, Rebecca blurted, "I was just kind of worried about you."

"You don't need to be."

"I noticed that you weren't talking to Katie or the other girls very much."

"Oh." Lilly rolled her eyes. "Katie's not happy with me."

"Why?"

"Peter's walked me home a couple of times. I think she wishes he was walking with her instead of me."

Rebecca felt like slapping a palm against her own forehead. Here she'd been so worried about the girl, grieving for her parents and struggling to fit in, when she was simply caught up in normal teenage drama. Leave it to Rebecca to put one and one together and come up with three.

Looking for something to say, Rebecca said, "I only know Peter a little bit from work. Is he nice?"

"I think so. He's been nice to me." She paused, then said, "Do you have a boyfriend?"

Rebecca was a little uncomfortable turning the conversation to herself, but she knew she shouldn't have been surprised that things had moved in that direction. If she was going to ask Lilly personal questions, it stood to reason that the girl would want to ask the same things about her. "*Nee*," she said at last. "I mean, not at the moment."

"But you have had one before?"

Rebecca had to think about that. Oh, she'd had crushes on different boys from time to time, but was never serious about any of them. "You know what, I haven't."

Lilly looked at her. "Why not?" Her voice wasn't sharp. Instead it was curious.

And it made Rebecca reflect on things, too. "I'm not really sure," she said with a shrug. "I don't think I really have a reason. I just always felt that it wasn't the right time."

"Oh." Lilly frowned and stared straight ahead again.

There she'd gone again. Messing something up that she should have taken more care with. The last thing she'd wanted to do was embarrass the girl.

Maybe it was time to switch topics. "So, how is your uncle doing?"

"Onkle Jacob? He's fine, I guess. Better than me."

"What's bothering you?"

"Other than the fact that both my parents died and I'm the new girl here? Not a thing."

"I'm sorry. I didn't mean to be insensitive."

The girl sighed. "You weren't. I'm sorry, I shouldn't have spoken to you like that."

"Would you like to talk about things? I'm a good listener."

Pure frustration lit the girl's features. "Miss Kinsinger, I don't know why you decided to walk with me but I'm okay. I don't need a new teacher friend."

Each word was harsh and laced with bitterness. But there was so much pain, too, that Rebecca realized she couldn't be upset by Lilly's rudeness. Instead, her heart went out to the girl. It was obvious that she was grieving.

"I'm sorry. I should've remembered your background. I spoke without thinking."

Lilly, with her auburn hair and green eyes, stared at her in confusion. Then, to her surprise, she flushed as if she was embarrassed. "Listen, I'm sorry I'm being mean. I just get tired of talking about myself."

She flinched. "You don't need to apologize. I . . . well, I just wanted you to know I cared." They were now on Main Street. In just a few minutes, Lilly would be at the store and Rebecca would be at the mill.

"Why? What difference does it make? No matter what you might think or feel, it won't change anything. No matter how sorry you are or how much I smile and try to get on, it won't bring them back. They're gone forever."

"I know." Taking a ragged breath, she forced herself to push through the pain. "Lilly, I'm sorry about your parents. I know how you must feel."

"Yeah, right."

"I do. Both of my parents are in Heaven, too."

But instead of looking like she was glad to meet someone who had experienced the same loss, she simply looked at her blankly. "Did your parents die suddenly in a car accident?"

"Well, *nee*. My mother died years ago. But my *daed*—"

"Were you forced to move out of your house and leave all of your friends during your last year of school?" Lilly interrupted.

"*Nee*, but—"

"And are you an only child living with grandparents who are old and an uncle who knows less about kids than pretty much anyone?"

"Of course not."

"Then you do not know how I'm feeling."

"You're right. I am sorry for trying to be your friend."

Lilly sighed impatiently. "Miss Kinsinger, like I said, I am sorry I'm being so rude. I appreciate you being nice, too. But the fact of the matter is that I would really rather not talk—"

"That's enough, Lilly," a deep voice called out.

Startled, both Lilly and Rebecca turned around to discover that Jacob, Lilly's uncle, was approaching.

The teenager groaned. "Great. Just when I thought this day couldn't get any worse . . . it did."

Rebecca was pretty sure she couldn't agree more.

# Chapter 7

Jacob's face was thunderous. So thunderous, Lilly looked alarmed.

And Rebecca had no idea how to make this whole fiasco of a conversation better.

"Lilly, you owe Miss Kinsinger an apology," he called out. "Right now."

Looking pained, Lilly said, "I was just doing that."

"I heard what you were sayin'. As apologies go, it was a mighty poor one," he stated as several other men and women passed them on the sidewalk. "Now, try it again."

When Lilly's eyes watered, Rebecca stepped in. "She doesn't need to try again," she protested, not wanting to make the awkward situation even worse than it already was. Not only had she brought up a sensitive subject, she'd brought it up without considering Lilly's privacy. She should have known better. "I overstepped myself."

"I doubt that. From what I overheard, you were only trying to be nice," Jacob said as he drew to a stop in front of both of them. "Apologize now, Lilly."

Frustration flashed in her eyes, but she dutifully did as he asked. "Like I said, I'm sorry."

Rebecca attempted to smile. "That's okay."

Jacob shook his head. "Not hardly. Lilly, your father raised you better than this. And don't you start telling me how he ain't around. Believe me, I know he's gone."

Oh, but this was terrible! Why hadn't she just left this girl alone? "Please, Jacob. I would really like to drop this conversation."

"She owes you better manners, Rebecca. Her parents raised her better than this, and her grandparents and I expect better of her, too. Being sad and angry at the world is no reason to be mean to everyone else."

Rebecca knew he had a point. But she also knew that she could have handled the teenager better. "Lilly, you don't owe me anything. I'll see you next week when I volunteer again."

After a long moment, Lilly nodded. "Okay," she whispered at last. Then she raised her chin to meet her uncle's gaze. "Oncle Jacob, I was going to go to the market to get Mommi's apples."

Visibly regaining his composure, Jacob nodded. "That sounds like a good idea." His voice far more quiet and patient now, he patted her shoulder. "Go on then. I'll catch up with you and wait for you outside the market, then we can walk to the farm together."

Without answering, Lilly strode down the street toward the store.

When he and Rebecca were alone, Jacob sighed. "I am sorry for the way she spoke to you. There is no excuse."

"Oh, I think there might be," she replied. "Jacob, I meant

what I said. I approached Lilly uninvited, started walking by her side even though I knew I was making her uncomfortable, and then proceeded to badger her with questions without even asking if she'd mind me talking to her. The poor girl was just trying to walk to the store."

"I hear what you're saying, but her behavior ain't your fault. Lilly needs to learn that she can't take out her hurt on everyone else." After a second's pause, he said, "She also needs to remember that she isn't the only person who has lost a loved one recently."

As she noticed a new thread of pain cross his features, Rebecca realized that she had forgotten that he'd lost a brother. "I am sorry about that."

"No need to feel sorry for me. I'm okay."

For the first time since she met him, she realized that he looked vulnerable. It was a bit incongruous; he was tall and well-built. He looked strong and healthy. Capable of tackling any task put in front of him. But maybe he needed a friend as much as his niece did. "If you ever want to talk about things . . ." she began, before turning silent. What was she doing? Offering to counsel him like she had tried to do with Lilly? "Never mind."

His green eyes sharpened. "Rebecca, what were you going to say?"

He'd gentled his tone. To her embarrassment, she felt herself responding to him in much the same way she had during their first meeting. "Oh, well . . . it was nothing," she stumbled.

"I'd still like to hear it. Please."

*Please.* That little word, combined with his intent gaze? Well, it was enough to make her flush.

Embarrassed by her reaction, she looked down at her blue

dress and realized that she'd managed to get some chalk smudged on her sleeve. She rubbed at the mark in order to gain a few seconds' time. "I was just gonna say that I am pretty good at listening, if you ever need an ear."

His gaze warmed. *"Danke."*

"You're welcome." She smiled . . . and there went her dimple.

Still staring at her intently, he swallowed. "About Lilly. I'll, ah, talk to her more this evening. I'm sure she'll be offering you a better apology soon."

"Jacob, please don't." Taking a chance, she said, "Actually, I think her getting upset with me might have done some good."

"Do you really think so? How?"

"Because she was telling me about herself and how she's feeling. Instead of keeping everything in, she was sharing. That's part of the grieving process."

He nodded slowly. "Perhaps you are right. Like I said, I've been grieving, myself. However, I hardly ever talk about my brother. It hurts too bad."

"It's all part of it, I think." After debating a moment, she decided to share. "Like I was telling Lilly, my father died recently, too. I'm one of four siblings and even though we're all adults, we've been having quite a time recovering from the loss. One of my brothers was really angry, too."

"I am sorry for your loss, too."

Taking another chance, she said, "How are you doing in Charm, Jacob? Are you settling in?"

He dropped his head, looking down at his work boots, which were coated with mud. After he took a moment, he looked up at her again. "Truth be told, I think I'm doing about as badly as my niece."

Her heart went out to him.

"I'm so sorry," she said. "Why are things going so badly? I thought you were living with your parents."

"I am." He glanced around, looking as if he wanted to speak precisely. "I love my parents and I get along with them fine." He paused. "Well, as well as any grown man would who hasn't lived in the same house as his parents for years."

She smiled. "I bet that has been an adjustment."

"You have no idea," he said with a smirk. "But unlike the rest of the family, I have no experience farming or of living outside Florida. My parents were raised here, moved to Pinecraft when my brother and I were mere babes, then moved back soon after Lilly was born. For the first five years they were here, Marc worked the farm by my father's side. Then, when Lilly got old enough for school, they moved to Annie's parents' farm over in Berlin."

She was finally beginning to understand his past. "So that is why Lilly is comfortable with farming but new to Charm."

"*Jah*. When Marc and Anne died, Lilly was kind of left in a bad spot. Anne's parents are about ten years older than mine. They didn't want to raise a thirteen-year-old."

"Which is why you came here."

He nodded. "Don't get me wrong, Rebecca. I want to be here. I want to raise Lilly. I love her. I want to help my parents, too. But I'm currently an exceptionally poor farmer and an even poorer substitute father." Looking just beyond her, he muttered, "I thought it would be easier."

She couldn't help but smile. His honesty was refreshing. "I am sorry about that."

He looked surprised at her expression. "What did I say that was amusing?"

"Nothing. I just couldn't help but compare your situation to mine. I'm trying to be a teacher but I'm not very good at it. Most of the time when I'm there, I watch the clock and look forward to when I can leave," she commented as they started to walk.

"Uh-oh." He grinned, and some of that same admiration she saw earlier in his eyes appeared again.

She wasn't the only person feeling that attraction between them.

She hoped she wasn't blushing again. "Uh-oh is right. Basically, I keep wondering why I am even trying."

"Lilly said you've been there a lot."

Rebecca wondered how he knew about that. Was Lilly sharing more or had Jacob been asking about her? "I have. I just wish my time there was easier."

"If it's so hard and it's making you so uncomfortable, why are you doing it? I mean, do you ever wonder why you are trying to do something over and over that you can't seem to figure out?"

"All the time. But there's something inside me that is afraid to give up. Teaching has been a dream of mine for years. I've always pushed it aside and put my family and the lumber mill first. I don't want to look back on this time in my life and wonder if I should have tried harder."

"I'm doing the same thing. I don't want to give up."

"Are your parents helping you?"

"Yep. They say I'm being too hard on myself. They say that farming is as much about luck as it is about experience."

"I'm fortunate in the fact that I have an understanding older brother. Lukas is now a big believer in following one's heart. He understands that each day is a gift."

"Now?" He glanced her way. "Is that because of the mill accident?"

"Maybe. It might also be that he and Darla Kurtz recently got married. They had quite a few obstacles between them but they followed their hearts instead of letting their fears guide them."

He chuckled. "Even I have heard about their sudden romance. He proposed at the post office, didn't he?"

She grinned. "Indeed, he did. Rumor has it that he locked the door and wouldn't let her leave until she said yes."

"That's just a rumor, is it?"

"That's what some say," she teased. With some surprise, she realized that they were standing right in front of the lumber mill's entrance. "It looks like you walked me all the way to work. Thank you."

"Don't thank me. Our conversation helped me a lot. Thanks for listening to me whine."

"I've done my share of whining from time to time and can promise you that you were not whining. There's nothing wrong with being honest."

"I guess not. Well, I'll let you get to work. You put in some long days."

"I do, but it's worth it. I want to spend time at Charm Amish School and follow my dream, if only for a little while."

Jacob glanced toward the store. Through the big plate-glass windows across the street, he could see that Lilly was at the checkout counter. "It looks like Lilly found my *mamm's* apples without a problem. I'll be seeing you soon."

"Yes. And don't worry. People tell me farming is a grueling job, even for the most experienced farmer."

"Thanks for that," he said with a sarcastic smile.

He had just turned to leave when the door to the mill opened and Lukas came out. "Jacob, wait," Rebecca called. When he turned, she held out a hand toward her brother. "This is Lukas. Lukas, this is Jacob Yoder. He just moved here from Florida."

Lukas held out his hand. "Good to meet you. What brought you to Charm?"

"My brother recently passed on to Heaven. I'm currently attempting to farm my family's land."

Lukas's brows rose. "Sounds like there's a story there. Are the farming methods in Ohio much different from down in Florida?"

He grimaced. "Let's just say that I'm not too good at farming in either state. I worked in construction in Sarasota."

Lukas smiled. "I've often been glad that God decided that I was born into a lumber mill family and not a farming one. If you ever decide that farming ain't for you, let me know. We hire a lot of construction workers."

"*Danke.*"

After they said good-bye again, Rebecca smiled. "Thanks for saying that."

"You're welcome, but I don't know what I did."

"Saying Jacob could come to you for a job if he needed one."

"I meant what I said. Construction workers are a natural fit for the mill. They are used to working with the materials and have a lot of knowledge about what works and doesn't." He frowned. "I hope he didn't take my offer as a sign that I didn't think he should farm, though."

She shook her head. "I think he was relieved to know that he had options. I'll tell you his story later, but suffice it to say that he's got his hands full."

Looking at her fondly, he nodded. "I think we all do." Stuffing his hands in his pockets, he said, "I'm going to head on out of here."

"You're going home?"

"Nope. I'm actually off to the Kurtz farm. Darla spent most of the day over there with Aaron and Patsy trying to get a handle on things."

"Has anything new happened?" Rebecca knew that Darla's siblings weighed heavy on her mind. Shortly after their father died in the fire at the mill, several people in town had laid all the blame on his shoulders.

Darla ended up working at the post office, in an attempt to stay so busy she had no time to dwell on her pain. Her brother Aaron had let his temper get the best of him. He was currently getting counseling from one of the preachers and concentrating on making amends.

On top of all that, their mother had abandoned them. Her grief, combined with the verbal abuse from people like Mary Troyer, had gotten to be too much for her, and she had simply taken off. She'd left a note saying that she needed a break from all of the demands of her life.

Of course, her abandonment had hit all the Kurtz siblings hard, most especially the youngest girls, Maisie and Gretel. Darla was trying her best. It was only because of Patsy's and Aaron's insistence that they wanted her to be happy that she'd agreed to marry Lukas recently.

"Nothing new has happened. It's just a lot for everyone to deal with," Lukas said.

"How's Aaron doing? Has he been able to work on his temper? Is he getting along with Hope?"

"I think he's doing okay. He seems like a new man, praise God." With a smile, he added, "Actually, he and Hope are doing much better. From what Darla tells me, he also seems to be mending his relationship with his other siblings. He and Darla are helping each other a lot. He's also glad to be farming. Unlike your new friend Jacob, I hear he's a natural farmer."

"Let me know if I can help in any way."

"You already do enough." Rocking back on his heels, he looked a bit shamefaced. "Sorry, but I left you a long list of things to do. I think Mercy left you some questions, too."

"Sounds like I better get inside and get busy."

"Becky, listen . . . everything doesn't have to get done today."

"I'll do as much as I can. Don't worry."

"Work until six, then come home, all right?"

"I can do that."

"See you tonight," he said before walking quickly down the sidewalk.

Rebecca watched him, his shoulders strong and proud. She couldn't help but compare him to Jacob. Where Lukas had light hair, cut short, and the faint beginnings of a beard, Jacob had Lilly's striking green eyes and dark brown hair. Jacob wasn't quite as tall and thickly muscled as Lukas, either. However, he was just as fit-looking. He was also clearly as devoted to his family as Lukas was.

And because of that, Rebecca knew she was intrigued by him. How many men would pick up their whole lives and make a go of it for a niece? Not many, she decided. While some men might even agree to raise their niece, they would have asked for the girl to join them, not the other way around.

What he was doing was really a wonderful thing.

Closing her eyes, she said a brief prayer for both of those men. For them both to find the strength they needed to help those who needed them to be strong.

And then, because she knew the Lord was always with her, she asked Him to give her a little bit of strength, too. She was going to need His help if she was going to tackle the mess that Mercy had no doubt left her.

Feeling better already, she opened the main door at last, felt the cool burst of air conditioning on her skin, and strode inside.

She was now ready to get to work and do her part for her family. At least she knew she was good at *this* job.

# Chapter 8

*Wednesday, August 26*

Even if Rachel's head wasn't exactly coming to terms with her pregnancy, her body surely was! She'd woken up nauseated for the last three days. She'd also been nauseated after dinner, after supper, and before she went to sleep. Her skin felt extra sensitive and she was tired, too.

That evening, after she'd gotten home from school, she'd chopped carrots, celery, and onions, put them in a pot with some chicken bouillon and water, and set it on the stove to boil. Now all she had to do was take out the dish of fresh chicken, cut it up, and add it to the broth so she could make chicken and dumplings for Marcus.

Unfortunately, even thinking about that raw chicken made her stomach turn to knots.

She took a seat on her favorite kitchen chair and tried to summon some of her mother's strength. She had carried five *kinner*. Surely Rachel could handle this first pregnancy!

She would handle it, too. In another minute or so. First, though, she needed to put her feet up and take a rest. Her students had been especially rambunctious today.

"Rachel?" Marcus called out. "Rachel, what in the world?"

She opened bleary eyes. Then, as reality set in, she scrambled to her feet guiltily. "Oh, Marcus. I'm sorry. I must have fallen asleep."

"With a pot on the stove, too."

Racing to the stove, she looked at the pot of vegetables. They didn't look too overcooked. Relief coursed through her. She must have been asleep for only a few minutes. "I'll get the chicken on."

"I'll take care of the chicken. You go sit back down."

Because she really, really didn't want to handle that icky wet chicken, she did as he bid. And sure enough, the moment he started cutting it up, her stomach rolled. With a groan and a cough, she rushed to the bathroom.

Two minutes later, Marcus found her sitting on the floor, her head resting against the cool tile wall. Before she knew what he was about, he slid down beside her, a warm washcloth in his hand. "Rachel, you are mighty sick."

"It's simply morning sickness."

"At five in the evening?" he asked as he handed her the washcloth.

After pressing the warm cloth against her mouth and cheeks, she tried to joke. "Mamm said *bopplis* don't know the difference between morning and evening."

"I guess not." After helping her to her feet, he walked her to their bed. "Come lie down."

"I don't have time for that. I need to make you supper."

"The chicken is cooking. I'm thinking it might be best if you stay out of the kitchen for a bit."

"You might be right." She did still feel a bit queasy.

He sat on the bed and took her hand. "Rachel, you being so tired and sick ain't good. Maybe we should take you to the doctor."

"Agnes says this is normal."

He frowned. "Agnes is as old as the hills."

"She's not that old. Plus, she knows a lot more about being pregnant than I do. We need to trust her."

"I haven't wanted to say anything, but I don't want her delivering our baby."

"Why not?"

"She's got to be seventy years old."

"That may be, but she still is capable. She delivered me and probably you, too."

"I don't know about that. Even if she did, she delivered us years ago. I think we need to go to someone else."

"Who?" Sure her husband wasn't thinking straight, Rachel added, "She's the *midwife*, Marcus."

"She's not the only option. I want you to go to a real obstetrician who delivers babies at the hospital."

"But I want to have my baby here at home. Just like my mother did."

"It's safer to be in the hospital."

"My mother did just fine." Though it was a struggle, she attempted to lighten the tension between them. "I am fine, too."

"That's not the point. We need to be prepared in case something goes wrong." His voice was strong and deep as he continued, oblivious to the look of dismay that was written on her face.

"But I am healthy. Nothing is going to go awry." Since he didn't look so sure, she added, "You know what, I'll ask my mother to be in the room, too."

"My mind is made up, Rachel. This is for the best. For both you and the baby." Before she could get in another word, he continued. "While we're talkin' about the future, I think you need to quit your job, too."

She relaxed. This, at least, she agreed on. "Of course I will. As much as I'm going to miss being in the classroom, I know that being a mother will be my most important job after the baby is here."

"To be sure. But it is your job now, too, *jah*? I fear it may be too tiring for ya. Rachel, dear, you need to take care of yourself."

"Now?" She examined his face. Tried to understand what was going through his mind. Usually, Marcus was easygoing, and he seemed proud of her teaching job.

"*Jah*, now. Being around all those *kinner* can make you sick. Or you could be on your feet too much." Sounding as if he'd just come up with the best idea ever, he said, "It's much better if you stay around here and rest."

She shook her head. "*Nee*, Marcus. I'm going to teach as long as I can."

"I don't want to argue with you. And I shouldn't have to. What I am saying makes sense. Ain't so?"

Actually, it didn't make any sense at all. At least not to her. Searching his face, she said, "Marcus, what is going on? Why are you so worried about my health and the baby?" Grasping at straws, she added, "Did something happen to your mother or your sister that I don't know about? Or . . . or is it about the mill? Are you thinking about the men at the mill?" She knew that he'd been affected by both the fire and the men's deaths. Yet, while some of the employees hadn't been shy about admitting how devastating the experience had been, Marcus had always insisted that he had gotten over it.

But maybe that hadn't been the case?

He moved from her side and got to his feet. "I am not going to talk about the fire."

"If you are still haunted by the experience, there's no shame in admitting it." Reaching out to him, she added, "I would be more than willing to talk about what happened that day."

"I would never burden you with such things."

"It wouldn't be a burden." Keeping her voice soft, she added, "It would mean that you need me as much as I need you."

His expression softened slightly. Then he blinked and it became hard once again. "This conversation is over. You can work the rest of the week, but then I expect you to be at home taking care of yourself."

For the first time since they'd exchanged vows, Rachel didn't intend to obey her husband. She needed to teach. It made her happy and it made her feel worthy.

Then, there was Lilly. That poor girl had already lost so much and was struggling to fit in. She'd only recently started to lose that haunted look in her eyes. What would happen to the girl if Rachel left? There was no guarantee that Rachel's replacement would treat Lilly with such care.

That settled it. Her mind was made up.

She had no intention of quitting her job. Somehow, some way, she was simply going to have to change Marcus's mind.

# Chapter 9

*Friday, August 28*

I still don't understand why you are walking with me to school, Uncle Jake," Lilly said when they were about halfway there. "I haven't done anything wrong."

Jacob wished Lilly was a little girl again. Or that he'd taken more time to get to know her over the years. Or that he was better with words. If he knew just the right words to say, she might actually want to talk to him about things that mattered to her.

If he'd done all that, then he would feel like he could stop walking and simply give her a hug. The poor thing was always preparing herself for the worst, and it was difficult to watch. Painful, even. It was becoming obvious that after experiencing so many upheavals, she now only expected bad news and disappointment in her future.

That was why he did his best to reassure her yet again. "I told you the truth. I promise, I did. All Mrs. Mast said was that she wanted to speak with me. I told her mornings were best. She said that time was *gut* because you *kinner* are busy with your morning routine. That's all there was to it."

"I understand the timing. But, *Onkle*, why did she want to see you *today*?"

"I don't know." Looking down at his niece, who was so obviously on the verge of tears, Jacob reached out and patted her on the back. "All we can do is visit with her like she asked. Surely she'll answer all our questions then."

"I hope so."

"I hope so, too." He smiled. "Now, let's try not to bring on problems. We'll deal with whatever Mrs. Mast has to say when the time comes."

With visible effort, Lilly regained control and started walking again. She shook her head wryly. "You know, Onkle Jacob, you could have met me at school. You didn't have to walk with me the whole way."

"What? You want me to walk by myself?" He raised his eyebrows and tried to look affronted.

His silly expression paid off. Lilly's lips twitched. "Maybe. Girls my age don't usually need grown-ups walking them places."

"That might be so, but I'm new at this, you know. You're simply gonna have to give me time to learn how to treat teenagers."

After she pretended to think about his words, her lips twitched again. "I suppose I can do that."

It took everything Jacob had to not grin or throw his fist in the air. Maybe he'd finally made a breakthrough with her. If it had actually happened, he was going to owe Mrs. Mast a big thank-you.

They were just past the last bend in the road. The white one-room schoolhouse loomed up ahead. Already several children were congregating outside. Some of the younger boys and girls were chasing each other. The oldest boys were standing off to one side talking. One girl was sitting on the steps reading.

And Rebecca Kinsinger was standing with two girls examining something in a textbook.

Just like that, his mind went blank. He couldn't explain it, but somehow whenever he saw her, he couldn't think about anything other than his need to get to know her better.

When Lilly started talking to one of the girls nearby, Jake took the opportunity to look at Rebecca, thankful that she couldn't see how intently he did so.

He supposed she looked like she always did. She had golden hair, light blue eyes, full cheeks. A winsome expression, and a loose, almost athletic build.

She reminded him of some women he'd met in Florida who were swimmers. A group of them spent a summer in one of the condo complexes he'd worked at and he'd gotten to know a couple of them. They'd be leaving for swim practice when he arrived early for work. They'd been tall, like Rebecca was. And they'd walked in such a fluid way, it had made him think that they were very comfortable with their bodies.

That was how Rebecca walked, forceful and assured. There was little hesitancy about her. In the few times their paths had crossed, he'd thought she seemed comfortable around most everyone, actually. He wondered if it was because of her job at the mill. She didn't have the usual shyness around men that most women seemed to have.

"Onkle Jacob," Lilly called out as she approached his side again.

"Hmm?" To his surprise, she nudged him with an elbow. It

interrupted his thoughts. In confusion, he stared down at her. "What was that for?"

"You're staring!" Lilly whispered.

He supposed he was. Jacob tilted his head and wondered if Rebecca's nose freckled in the sun or if it always stayed so flawless and perfect.

"Jacob," Lilly said a little louder. "You're staring at Miss Rebecca. She's gonna notice if you don't stop soon."

Quickly, he averted his eyes. "It was that obvious?"

"Kind of." For the first time all morning, Lilly smiled broadly. "You looked like you were mooning over her."

That was probably because he was. "Huh. I hope she didn't notice."

"I don't think so. She's still looking at the history book with Martha. Martha keeps getting the dates of the Civil War mixed up." She shook her head. "Martha can't remember anything that doesn't have to do with her farm. She's raising goats."

"Why does she need to know the dates?"

Lilly shrugged. "I don't know. It's not like any of us Amish girls are ever gonna start telling the corn all about the Battle of Gettysburg."

"You might," he teased. "If you thought it might help ya get a better crop."

In true thirteen-year-old fashion, she rolled her eyes. "I love you, Onkle Jake, but you tell the worst jokes."

Figuring she might be right, he turned his attention back to Rebecca and Martha. "Martha looks about your age."

"She is."

"Then how come she's studying with Rebecca? Do you have a history test today?"

"*Jah.*"

"You do? Did you study?"

"I didn't need to."

"Of course you do. Studying is important." He was starting to have a good idea of why Lilly's teacher wanted to talk to him.

"Unlike Martha, I know the Battle of Gettysburg was in 1863."

"Huh." Jake didn't get much of a chance to ask more questions because they were now in the middle of the playground. A couple of the kids watched them approach.

When Jacob noticed a few teenagers around Lilly's age look at him curiously, he said, "You don't have to stay with me, Lilly. Have a good day."

She practically sighed in relief. "You too, Onkle." She paused. "Hey, Onkle Jacob?"

"Hmm?"

"If Mrs. Mast tells you something bad, let me know right away, wouldja?"

"I will, honey. Try not to worry, okay?"

After nodding, Lilly turned away and approached a couple of kids her age. Jacob was happy to see that all the kids greeted her with smiles. Maybe she was making friends after all.

Just then the front door of the school opened, and Mrs. Mast came out. She rang a bell and ushered the kids inside.

Instead of going in right away, Rebecca turned to him. "Hi, Jacob."

"Hi. It's *gut* to see you." There, he sounded completely normal. Not moony at all. "I didn't know you were going to be volunteering here today."

Stepping closer, her expression warmed. "Rachel told me that you had a meeting with her this morning. I thought I'd come help her so she wouldn't keep getting interrupted."

"That's nice of ya."

She looked embarrassed. "It was nothing."

He disagreed, but he didn't want to embarrass her further. "So . . . do you know what the meeting is about?"

"I think so."

Now something bright shone in her blue eyes. It made him feel moderately relieved. Maybe this wasn't going to be the crisis he had imagined. "Care to share? Worrying about this meeting kept me up all night. Lilly's worried, too."

"I'm sorry you couldn't sleep, but you're going to have to wait for Rachel to get your answers."

"Sure?"

"Positive. I don't want to overstep things, you see." She smiled.

"Of course not." He smiled back. And as he did so, it occurred to him then that they were flirting. Nothing too overt or intense, but there was something new flowing between them. Part of him was relieved that the attraction he'd felt for her wasn't one-sided.

The other part hated the timing. His life was currently a mess. He was in a new place, living with his parents, and attempting to gain the trust of a niece he barely knew.

As they started walking up the stairs into the building, he said, "Listen, before I forget, I wanted to thank your brother for what he said. It's good to know that I could work at the mill if things don't work out on the farm."

"Things still aren't working out?" she asked gently.

"So far they aren't. I keep thinking that I'm going to get the hang of farming, but right now it seems like a lost cause."

"I bet it's not quite that bad."

"*Nee*, it is. The other day I broke the plow." Though it was embarrassing, he forced himself to continue. "I also put weed killer on some crops and used too much of the wrong type of fertilizer on the vegetable garden."

Her eyes widened. "You did not."

"I did. I had no idea that my father favored special fertilizer on his tomatoes. I thought he was going to kill me."

As he'd hoped, she giggled. "He wouldn't have done that. But you do sound rather hopeless."

Lowering his voice, he said, "I canna even believe I'm telling you this, but I hate it, too. I want to learn to be a *gut* farmer, but it's a hard road. Every hour seems to pass like it's two days long."

"I know the feeling," she murmured as they walked inside.

Immediately, Jacob felt like he was in the middle of an intricate timepiece. Each of the children seemed to be doing his or her own assignment. They were working separately but in tandem, too. Some were talking quietly with each other, others were working intently on whatever task was at hand.

"Hi, Jacob," Rachel Mast said as she approached. "It's good to see ya. *Danke* for meeting me early this morning."

Her casualness made him feel even more at ease. "Thanks for allowing me to visit."

"It wasn't any trouble. Besides, Rebecca here volunteered to help out." Looking at her fondly, Rachel said, "She's been a lifesaver."

"I've been glad to lend a hand," Rebecca said. "It not only helps you but gives me practice."

"I'm going to take Jacob outside. Let them have about another ten minutes to do their morning chores, then give the spelling test, okay?"

"Got it," Rebecca replied as she turned back to the children. "All right, everyone. We all have work to do. Let's see who can get it done first."

As Rachel led the way outside, she chuckled.

"Something funny?" Jacob asked.

"*Nee.* I just can't help but wonder how Rebecca will be when she gets her own classroom. She reminds me a bit of her bulldog puppy, Oscar."

Jacob thought that was an odd comparison. "Oh?"

"She approaches things head-on, without any doubts. When she stumbles, she simply gets right up and continues on."

"I'm beginning to think that is an apt description. She's seems exuberant."

"Oh, she is. I'm learning a lot from her." Looking around, she said, "Let's go sit over at the picnic table. I promise, I won't keep you long."

As they sat down, Jacob realized that he was nervous. Ready to get to the heart of the matter, he looked at her directly. "Mrs. Mast, what did you want to talk with me about?"

She raised her hands as if to calm him down. "It's nothing bad. Actually, it's something good."

Her expression looked the complete opposite of her words. She looked a bit worried. "I would be more reassured if you looked happier about that."

"I am happy, Jacob. I just . . . Well, I guess I'm procrastinating. I don't want to say the wrong thing."

"What is it? Is Lilly making friends?"

"She is. Not a lot, but that's okay. She's kind of a quiet girl. My impression is that she doesn't need or want to be in the middle of every conversation or group."

"That sounds about right. Lilly is kind of a self-contained sort of person."

"It takes all kinds of people to make a community, I think. Of course, I am just getting to know her, but my sense is that she's still grieving and a little bit wary of getting too close to anyone, given her circumstances. That said, she is doing fine socially."

"So, if it's not her friends, what is wrong?"

"She's smart."

Jacob raised his eyebrows. "Mrs. Mast, I'm still not following you. I've always thought being smart was a *gut* thing."

She chuckled. "Please, call me Rachel. And being smart is *gut*. What I'm trying to say is that your Lilly isn't just bright, she's really smart. Gifted."

"Gifted?" He was trying to keep up, but he felt a bit like she was speaking another language.

"At first, I thought that she was simply ahead of us. But when I questioned her about the things she'd been learning in Berlin, they didn't sound all that different from the curriculum here. So, I talked to her old teacher."

"Miss Wallace?"

"Yes. I talked to her a couple of days ago. And listening to her answered a lot of questions. She'd noticed how well Lilly read and wrote, too. And how inquisitive she was." Bracing her hands on the bench on either side of her light blue dress, she added in a dry tone, "And, how skilled she was in math."

"All of that?"

"*Jah.*" She chuckled. "I'm not exaggerating, Jacob. Actually, I think Lilly might be the smartest girl I've ever taught."

"That's *gut*, right?"

"It's good for me, but the reason I wanted to talk to you is that I think we need to make sure she gets some extra help."

Now he was really confused. "Why does Lilly need help if she's doing so good?"

"Because my job as a teacher is to take her from one place and help guide her toward another." She sighed. "I love teaching in a one-room schoolhouse. But in some cases, like with Lilly's, I fear that I am not able to do enough." Looking determined, she said, "Her success is important to me. I want her to feel secure and happy."

He wanted those same things. "What do you want to do?"

She bit her lip. "I wanted to talk to you in the hopes that you would, perhaps, allow me to contact some Englishers to tutor her in other subjects."

"Like who? I don't know how to even go about such things." And was that even a good idea? Was that what his brother would have wanted for Lilly? Maybe Marc had never wanted Lilly to be challenged.

"I thought I'd ask at the high school. Sometimes older students will tutor younger kids. Or you could also hire an Englisher tutor. Someone who has had more schooling than me."

Jacob was at a loss for words. As far as he could tell, Lilly's dream was to simply be done with school. But was that because she didn't like learning? Or was it that she'd just become bored.

Then, there were her grandparents. They were traditional people. What would they say about Lilly's need for more schooling? Would they fuss at him? Or, worse, at her? That would be devastating for her.

Rachel didn't look surprised about his sudden silence. "I know this is a lot to take in. That is one of the reasons why I wanted to talk to you right now. Take some time and think about what you and Lilly want to do. Talk to her about all this. She might have some ideas."

"Do you think she even realizes how smart she is?"

"I imagine so. But that doesn't mean she's completely comfortable with it, or thinks it is a good thing. She might simply be used to understanding things quickly and feels like she is supposed to wait until everyone catches up."

Jacob thought that would be a terrible way to go through each day. "I hope that's not what is happening."

"Me, too." Standing up, she brushed off her dress, then reached out to balance herself against the table.

"Are you all right?"

"Oh, for sure. I just got a little dizzy standing up too quickly." Once some of the color returned to her cheeks, she started walking back to the schoolhouse. "Why don't you send me a note when you're ready to make some plans? While you're doing that, I'll investigate some more options."

"You don't mind?"

"It's not only my job, it's my pleasure! Lilly's gifts are a wonderful challenge for me. I'm looking forward to helping her as much as possible."

"*Danke*. Thanks for caring."

"You're welcome, Jacob." As a roar floated out through the front door, she grimaced. "I think I had better get inside."

"*Jah*. It looks like our bulldog might need some help."

She grinned. "You said that, not me!"

# Chapter 10

*That same day*

When Mrs. Mast came back into the classroom, Lilly felt almost every eye in the room on her. She slumped down farther in her chair. *Great.* Now all the kids thought she was in trouble, too. It made sense. Why else would her uncle Jake be asked to come in to talk with Mrs. Mast during class?

But that said, for the life of her, she couldn't think of anything she'd done wrong.

Still pretending to read her book, Lilly eyed Mrs. Mast. After stopping to talk to some of the youngest members of the class, she chatted with Miss Kinsinger.

Then her teacher eyed Lilly in a thoughtful way.

After meeting her gaze, Lilly peered back at the open page in her lap. What had she done?

"Scholars, while Miss Kinsinger is here, I'm going to be visiting with each of you individually. When I call your name, bring me your homework."

The room erupted in a flurry of paper shuffling as the rest of the class attempted to get all of their things in order. Lilly pretended to organize her papers as well, though she'd done all her homework yesterday before she left.

"Anson, bring me your work, please."

"Oh, man," Anson groaned under his breath as he shuffled forward. Anson was eight and seemed like he'd rather be hunting for frogs than concentrating on what he was supposed to be doing. Lilly hid a smile. She didn't blame the freckle-faced, towheaded boy one bit. Frogs were far more interesting than spelling lists.

"Hey, Lilly," Katie whispered from her right.

*"Jah?"*

"What did your uncle want to talk to Mrs. Mast about?"

"I'm not sure. It wasn't his idea to come up here. She sent for him."

"She did? Oh, no! What did you do?"

After glancing to make sure that both adults in the room were otherwise occupied, she shrugged. "I don't know."

"Huh."

*"Jah.* I wish Mrs. Mast would just come out and tell me," Lilly said as Anson walked back to his chair.

After smirking at Anson, Katie leaned close again. "You just started at this school. Mrs. Mast always gives everybody second and third chances when they mess up. At least she does whenever I do something wrong. I bet it ain't nothing bad."

"I hope not," Lilly confided. But then again, she figured if Mrs. Mast had been happy with Lilly, she would have simply come out and told her. In her experience, only bad news was kept secret.

"Lilly, bring me your homework," Mrs. Mast called out.

The lump in her throat just got bigger. "*Jah*, Mrs. Mast." After gathering her assignments together quickly, she strode forward. She really hoped the whole class couldn't tell that her face was bright red.

When she got to Mrs. Mast's desk, Lilly carefully set her papers on the empty space in front of her teacher. "Here you go."

Mrs. Mast picked them up. When she said nothing more, Lilly turned to leave. "*Nee*, stay here, please."

Feeling even more ill at ease, Lilly stood silently and watched Mrs. Mast scan one paper after another.

All too soon, Mrs. Mast set the papers down with a sigh. Then she looked at Lilly in a direct way. "How long did these assignments take you last night?"

"Oh, well . . ." She allowed her voice to drift off. Because, of course, she hadn't actually done any of those papers the night before. She didn't want to lie, but she didn't want an honest answer to get her into further trouble.

Her teacher continued to stare intently. Then she cleared her throat. "That wasn't a difficult question to answer, Lilly. How long did this homework take you?"

There was no way she could lie to Mrs. Mast now. "I . . . Well, I didn't actually do any of that work last night."

"Oh? When did you do it?"

"Yesterday before the end of school."

"I see."

"I wasn't sneaking around," she added in a rush. "I just . . . Well, I had some time."

After searching her face again, Mrs. Mast said, "You finished your classwork early. Didn't you?"

Feeling miserable, Lilly nodded.

"And this happens a lot, doesn't it?"

"*Jah*. I'm sorry."

But instead of looking angry, Mrs. Mast looked kind of amused. "There's nothing to apologize for, Lilly. I've noticed that you are a hard worker, but that you seem to have a difficult time working hard in this classroom."

"I wouldn't say that. I'm doing okay."

"Well, let's be honest. The fact is that my assignments are too easy for you. You are not getting enough work to challenge your mind. That's not good."

To admit that she found the work too easy seemed like she was bragging. "It's not just your class. It's always been that way."

"I thought that might be the case. That's why I gave your old teacher a call. She said you were her star pupil, too."

"Really?" Miss Wallace had never acted like she was a star. Instead, she'd always seemed a bit put out with her.

"Really. That's why I asked your uncle to come in this morning to talk to me, Lilly. I think we need to work out a new plan for you."

"What kind of plan?"

"A plan where you are challenged more. There's no reason for you to be doing sixth-grade math when you should be doing eighth-grade or high school studies. I'm going to make up some assignments just for you."

"How?"

Mrs. Mast leaned back. After glaring at two of the older boys who were whispering to each other, she said, "I'm not exactly sure, to be honest. There are some personal things I need to take care of in addition to schoolwork, so I need to think about this for a little bit. But don't worry, Lilly. We're going to make this classroom the right fit for you. I want you happy here."

Lilly's eyes teared up. It was something little, but it meant so much. Maybe, just maybe, she was going to finally fit in at school. And if that happened, she might have something good to grab ahold of.

If she couldn't have her parents anymore, she had to have something to hold on to.

Immediately, Mrs. Mast looked distressed. "I'm so sorry, dear. You've been through so much and now I'm giving you even more to think about. I had hoped this would alleviate some worries, but I'm guessing it's also a lot to take in."

"I'm fine."

Still studying her carefully, she lowered her voice. "You're not fine. You know what? Why don't you step outside and take a moment."

"I don't want to go out there by myself." Could there be anything worse than having the whole class know that she needed to take a break first thing in the morning?

"I'll go out there with her," Peter volunteered.

Both Mrs. Mast and Lilly started. "Peter," Mrs. Mast said, "I didn't see you standing there."

His attention still focused on Lilly, he shrugged. "I saw she was upset."

Mrs. Mast looked at him carefully. "Did you do your homework last night?"

"*Jah.*"

"Set it on my desk, then please take Lilly outside for ten minutes."

Lilly looked at her teacher in surprise.

Mrs. Mast shrugged. "I've got a soft spot for that boy. He's my nephew. And he's almost done with school. He would be a good friend to you, Lilly."

For some reason, those words of kindness made her tear up all over again. "*Danke*, Mrs. Mast," she said.

Just then, Peter set a pile of papers on his aunt's desk, then smiled Lilly's way. "Come on," he said.

As she followed Peter down the aisle between the desks and out the door, she tried not to catch anyone's eye. It was bad enough that she could feel everyone's attention on the two of them. She was certain that as soon as she got back to the room, Katie was going to ask her a hundred questions.

Once they were outside, she breathed a sigh of relief. "*Danke*, Peter. I really needed to get out of there."

"No need to thank me. I'm always looking for a way to get out of class." Glancing around, he said, "Come on."

She followed him down the school's front steps, past the picnic tables, and finally to the swings. "You want to swing?" she asked.

"Not particularly. But I don't want to sit in front of the windows. Every person inside will watch us."

"I guess you have a point." She sat down and curled her hands around the chain holding up the swing. "I can't believe Mrs. Mast let us leave for a few minutes. My old teacher would've never let me do this."

"I'm not all that surprised. My aunt Rachel is really nice. And besides, you looked pretty upset."

"I guess I was."

"Want to talk about it? Was it why your uncle had to come up to school today?"

"*Jah*. Mrs. Mast—I mean your aunt—"

"You can call her Mrs. Mast. I do when I'm here."

"Well, anyway. She . . . Well, she noticed that I am having an easy time in school."

"*Nee.*"He smiled. "She noticed that you're really, really smart."

"*Jah.*" She kept her gaze straight ahead. "I don't know why book learning is so easy for me. It just is."

"If I tell you something, will you promise not to get mad?"

"Peter, you've been walking me home for weeks and you just rescued me from bursting into tears in front of the entire class. I won't get mad."

"Aunt Rachel talks about you to my parents."

"What does she say?"

"She thinks you're special."

"I'm not that," she protested quickly. She did not want anyone feeling sorry for her because her parents died. And she really didn't want anyone noticing that schoolwork came easy for her. She just wanted to fit in.

"Lilly, don't get all upset," he cajoled. "Please, just listen to me. She says that when the Lord gives a person a brain like yours, it needs to be nurtured. She is really excited about helping you."

Her eyes filled up with tears again.

He noticed. Hopping off his swing, he grabbed ahold of one of her chains, keeping her in place. "Hey. What just happened?"

"My last teacher never made me feel good. She always acted like I was bragging or something."

Peter's eyebrows rose. "She shouldn't have made you feel bad because God made you smart."

"I don't know about that."

"All right. How about you shouldn't feel bad because you're smarter than the rest of us?"

She still didn't like how that made her sound. "I'm only book smart. You are smart in a lot of other ways. You even have a *gut* job. That's pretty special."

For the first time since she'd met him, Peter looked unsure. "I don't think so."

"I do." Taking a fortifying breath, she said, "I can't believe how different everything is here in Charm. Even my parents never really understood how I've felt about school. They loved me, of course. But they didn't want me to do anything different. I started hiding the things that I was working on. Your aunt and even my uncle Jake—and now you . . . well, all of you make me feel like I don't have to be ashamed."

"You don't have anything to be ashamed about, Lilly. There's nothing wrong with you."

She smiled at him. "*Danke.* I hope you don't think I'm complaining." She stopped abruptly. She was though, wasn't she?

Peter shook his head. Somehow, even while shaking his head he looked confident and self-assured. "Stop worrying so much. Everything that's happening is good."

"You're so confident. I wish I was that confident."

"Then stick with me," he said with a laugh. "You'll get the hang of it."

"Sure I will," she muttered, taking care to make sure he heard the sarcasm in her voice. She and he both knew she'd never be as self-assured as he was.

Still grinning, he said, "All right. If you don't think you can ever be as confident as me, then trust me instead. I think it's great."

She smiled softly. "Thanks for being my friend."

"I'm glad I'm your friend. I promise."

"Lilly? Peter?" Miss Kinsinger called out. "It's time to come in now."

"Right here!" Peter yelled. "We better get inside."

He waited until she hopped off the swing, then walked beside her all the way back. And when they got to their seats and everyone was staring at them, Peter glared at them all so they'd stop. His behavior wasn't very nice, but Lilly secretly liked that he was trying to protect her. She liked it a lot. Ever since her parents died she'd felt more than a little alone. As if everyone around her was in charge and she'd had no choice but to follow along.

Today had felt different, though. She felt older. More assured. And maybe, just maybe, like she was going to one day be okay.

# Chapter 11

*Thursday, September 3*

August was a memory.

The corn had been harvested and plowed under a month ago. Now they were waiting for the timing to be right to bale hay.

And while the new rhythm of his life was feeling easier, Jacob wasn't finding any more enjoyment in his new occupation than he had last week or the week before that. It was too bad, too, because he actually did enjoying spending so much time with his father. He didn't, however, enjoy feeling like a bumbling child around him.

After years of being in charge of a carpentry crew, Jake was now his father's student, dutifully listening as he imparted advice.

Today, after his *daed* had answered Jacob's many questions with more patience than Jacob had ever thought possible, the two of them had gone into the barn and repaired one of the horse stalls. That had been the first time all day that Jake had felt like himself. He'd slipped on his worn leather work gloves, felt the length of wood for weaknesses, then expertly fitted new lumber into place.

His father had watched him in silence, only nodding from time to time. His intense stare made Jacob wonder what his father was thinking. Did he feel relief that his son was finally doing something without needing an explanation first? Or was he merely wishing that Jacob could wield a hoe as well as a hammer?

Afterward, when his father had gone back to the pastures, presumably to make sure they hadn't left any tools behind, Jacob had lent his mother a hand. She'd been working in her garden all day digging up potatoes and carrots. She'd been grateful for his company and kept up a lively, one-sided conversation, filling him in on her neighbors' and friends' antics while he brushed grasshoppers and other assorted bugs from his arms and face.

By six o'clock, his body was sore, his skin felt like it was covered in a fine layer of dust, and he was thoroughly disgruntled. Though he enjoyed the time with his parents, it was becoming more and more apparent that he was never going to be a decent farmer. He was definitely not the gifted farmer his father and his brother had been.

Perhaps just as important, he wasn't sure if he ever wanted to be. He didn't care for farming. He now understood that it wasn't that he was ill-suited for the job; he simply detested it. The Lord had been wise to plant him in Pinecraft for the first part of his life.

"You seem pretty quiet today, son," his *daed* said as they washed up at the spigot outside before heading into the house to shower. His mother hated dirt tracked on her clean wood floors.

"Do I?" He shrugged. "Must be the heat."

"It's only seventy degrees out. It ain't the heat, Jacob. What's on your mind?"

"Nothing." Well, nothing he wanted to talk to his father about. Daed had enough burdens to bear. After running his forearms under the faucet's spray, Jacob stepped back so his father could do the same.

As his *daed* turned off the faucet, he looked at Jake intently. "Are you worried about Lilly and what her teacher had to say?"

"*Nee*. I'm happy for her. And relieved. I was so worried Mrs. Mast was going to tell me that Lilly wasn't adjusting. Being too smart for her grade is a good thing, I think."

"I'm inclined to agree. When you first told your mother and me about this, we weren't sure what to think. Marc had never acted like Lilly was anything but an average girl." He frowned. "But now I'm wondering if Anne and Marc simply chose to pretend she was."

Jacob hated to think anything negative about his brother, but he thought that might be the case. Marc had been excellent at being productive. He'd made lists of tasks and checked them off when they were accomplished.

But Jacob had a feeling that Lilly's special gifts might have really thrown his brother for a loop.

"I guess the Lord's timing is working perfectly again," Jake mused. "He put Lilly in Mrs. Mast's class and in my care, too. Even though I'm not her *daed*, I am of the mind to help her develop her special talents instead of simply fitting in."

"Well said, son." After stretching his arms, his father placed his straw hat back on his head, brushed off the worst of the dust from his clothes, and led the way back to the house.

Years ago, Marc and Daed had come across a pallet of old bricks. They'd taken it home and fashioned a pretty red walkway from his mother's garden to the house. Over time, his mother had planted dozens and dozens of perennials along its edges. It was a beautiful walkway and fitting for his very kind and lovely mother. As they walked along it, Jacob realized that his mother had been meant to be a gardener and housewife. She kept a pretty, neat-as-a-pin home.

It made it clear that the Lord had given each of them special gifts that were meant to be used. "Daed, I am starting to get the feeling that Lilly has been covering up her talents."

Just outside the back door, his *daed* bent down and unlaced his heavy work boots. "We need to figure out why that is," he said. "It would be a shame if Lilly thought that we weren't going to be proud of her, no matter what. I hope she soon realizes that we simply want her to be happy. It don't matter to me if she goes a different path than I did or her parents intended."

Jacob was glad they were on the same page. "*Jah.* I agree."

Something flickered in his father's eyes. "I'm glad you do, son."

Right before Jacob opened the door, he looked at his father curiously. "Why am I getting the feeling that you are talking about something more than Lilly?"

"Maybe I am."

"I've been out in the fields all day. I'm hot, dirty, and tired. I don't know if I'm up for playing a guessing game."

"I'm not playing a game with you, Jake." But yet again he was staring at Jacob as if there was something mighty important to be read between the lines.

"Father, what are you needing me to understand?" he asked impatiently.

"I simply want you to think about yourself, son. Think about your gifts and what you might be hiding now."

"What did I do?"

His father didn't crack a smile or look put off by Jacob's terse tone. "You moved here, took on the care of a teenaged girl, and now are trying to be a farmer."

"*Jah*. So?" He couldn't imagine why his father would have a problem with any of that. He'd dropped everything for his family. Once more, he'd done it willingly and with an open heart.

"Ack, but you have always been like this. You never could see the forest for the trees."

Jacob's mind was so muddled, he was having a difficult time following him. But he sensed his *daed*'s words were important. Really important.

Frustrated with himself, Jacob lost it. "What? What are you trying to say, Daed?"

"That I see what you are doing. You're attempting to become something you're not meant to be. Furthermore, it's a poor fit, son. There is a reason you were happy down in Florida doing carpentry work. I don't want to be unkind, but you, Jacob, are a mighty poor farmer."

"Daed, I don't know what to say. I moved here to help you and Mamm. I wanted to help with Lilly."

"I know you did."

"And I moved here to be closer to you. It will always be a regret of mine that I didn't stay in better contact with Marc and Anne."

"I am aware of that, too." Taking off his worn straw hat again, his father ran a hand through his brown hair. It was a gesture that Jacob had witnessed hundreds of times growing up. It was an act that signaled his *daed* was running out of patience. More than that, he was weary. A sure sign that his father was tired of talking and had nothing else to say.

"Do you want me to figure the rest of this out on my own?" Jacob asked.

"If you want. But just remember that you and Lilly have more in common than you think. Each of you is afraid to show the world the person you really are because you don't want to disappoint. But what you have to understand is that neither of you is making anyone happy when you try to be something you ain't."

Slapping his hat back on his head, his father said, "Be the person God meant you to be, Jacob. If you do that, everything else will fall into place."

"I'll . . . I'll talk to Lilly about that tonight."

"*Gut.*" His father smiled softly. "That is a *gut* start, son."

"And . . . and I'll do some thinking about who the Lord has intended for me to be all along."

"That is an even better start," he replied. Then, as Jacob stood in the doorway, his father pushed by him and strode inside.

# Chapter 12

*Friday, September 4*

After double-checking that no one was around, Rebecca called out, "Hiya, turtles. It's a *gut* day out. Ain't so?"

Of course they didn't reply. She never expected that! But she did kind of think that her little friends in this pond were happy to hear from her.

There wasn't a real good reason why Dawdi Pond had always made her so happy. It wasn't much. Some people in and around Charm and Sugarcreek had ponds that could probably be called lakes, they were so large. This one wasn't. But it was within easy walking distance, and it had a nice bank with just enough rocks so that Rebecca could sit on there and never get the seat of her dress smudged with dirt or mud. And it froze quickly in the winter, which meant she could skate on it for months. She loved that. She loved putting on her favorite blue mittens and gliding across the ice, feeling as free and nimble as the birds that flew over it.

But she loved the pond most of all because a sapling had fallen across the middle of it when she was a young girl . . . and that's where the turtles now liked to sit.

Rebecca didn't really understand it, but she loved those turtles. She liked to count them resting in a row, their green and brown shells lined up neatly like jars on a shelf. She loved when their little green heads poked out. Sometimes they stretched them toward the sun. And sometimes—she was sure of it—they stretched them toward her so they could see her.

Whenever they were out, Rebecca would gather up the skirts of her dress, perch on the edge of a rock, and watch them. And they, in turn, watched her. Their beady black eyes always looked so serious. So intent.

When she was a little girl, she used to pretend that they could read her mind. When she was old enough to go to the pond by herself, she would talk to them.

Now that she had little Oscar to look after, she talked to him. But sometimes he got tired of hearing about her day and began rooting around in the weeds for good things to eat before taking a nap. Rebecca decided that bulldogs were mighty cute and good to cuddle . . . but they had far shorter attention spans than a row of box turtles.

"Hey!" She started at the sound of Lukas's voice. "I thought I'd find you here," he said as he strode forward along the bank.

"Luke, it's close to eight. Why are you out here?"

He shrugged. "After you left to take Oscar for a walk, Amelia asked Darla if she'd go deliver some more casseroles with her."

"Do you mind?" Rebecca had a feeling that sometimes Lukas and Darla wished they had more time to spend alone together.

"Nah, I didn't mind at all. Amelia needs some company, and I think Darla is having fun getting to know her better."

"I can see that. Darla and I were always better friends because we're close to the same age. We used to tell Amelia to leave us alone."

"I did the same with Levi." He winced, as he always did whenever he mentioned their brother.

"Well, Oscar got tuckered out so I decided to give him a little rest before heading home."

Lukas grinned. "*Nee*, I think you decided to visit with your turtle friends and Oscar got bored."

She was slightly offended. Okay, she was slightly embarrassed. "I don't have turtle friends."

"You talk to turtles, Becky. They also stare right at you."

She couldn't help but be pleased that he noticed. "They kinda do, don't they?"

"I heard you speaking to them when I walked around the bend."

She didn't bother to deny it—though she wished she'd spied him earlier. "They are good listeners." She shrugged. "They never talk back or interrupt."

"Sounds like we could all learn from them." He smiled. "Did you figure out whatever was bothering you?"

"Maybe."

"Want to share?"

"I don't want to burden you, Luke."

Sitting down on the ground, he picked up Oscar and deposited him on his lap. As the puppy wiggled and cuddled closer, Lukas petted him absently. "You don't have to tell me a thing. But if you'd like to, I'd like to hear it."

Glancing his way, Rebecca noticed that he was watching her in an expectant way. He really was hoping she'd share her burdens with him . . . just like he'd shared his fears a few months ago when he was so worried about his relationship with Darla.

That's what love was, she remembered. A give-and-take. Being brave enough to share, even when those things that are shared don't present oneself in the best light.

With that in mind, she plunged forward. "The truth is that I've been kind of worried, Lukas."

"About?"

"About my big dream."

"I know what that is. Your dream of becoming a teacher."

*"Jah."* Staring at the turtles, she said, "I've always kind of resented the fact that Mamm and Daed never took my dream of wanting to be a teacher seriously. I felt that Daed had his dream of owning the lumber mill and running it. But it was so demanding, he kind of just expected the rest of us to want his dream, too."

"I can see your point," he said slowly. "He had me up there helping out and doing odd jobs from the time I was ten. He honestly didn't allow me to think that my future would be anything but the mill."

Rebecca had never heard Lukas actually admit that. "Did that bother you?"

He shook his head. *"Nee.* I wanted that, too. I wanted to run it." Looking embarrassed, he added, "That said, I never wanted to take it over at this age."

"I know that. Everyone knows that."

"I hope so," he mused. "But to answer your question, I guess my dream was what our father wanted it to be." He paused, then added, "Rebecca, it's okay to want to be a teacher. You shouldn't feel bad that you are now getting the opportunity to help out in the classroom because Mamm and Daed died. They would have let you do it. They would have never stood in the way of that."

"I know."

He tilted his head. "So what's bothering you? Are you wishing that you were the teacher now?"

"*Nee*, that's not it."

"Then what is it?"

She couldn't put it off any longer. "Lukas, the problem is that I am not a very good teacher."

"You've already told me this. Why are you bothered now?"

"I'm bothered because I've really been trying hard to improve. Unfortunately, it's not working. I'm not good with all those *kinner*."

"I'm sure you're fine."

It was time to be brutally honest, with both herself and him. "*Nee*, I'm not."

"You haven't been trying all that long. Only a few weeks. No one gets good at anything in just a few weeks."

She supposed he had a point. But still. "I don't know."

"Becky, you will be a *gut* teacher one day," he stated in his usual confident way. Then he looked at her carefully. "That is, if that's what you want to happen."

He'd hit the nail on the head.

"That's the problem. You see, I'm starting to think that maybe I don't want to be a *gut* teacher."

All his confidence drifted into confusion. "I'm sorry, Becky, but you've lost me."

She knew the feeling! She'd been feeling pretty lost herself. After giving herself a moment to collect her thoughts, she said,

"Lukas, today, when I was at school, all I could think about was that I was ready to get out of there."

"Because?"

"Because I didn't know what to say to some of those scholars of Rachel's! A couple of the boys and girls asked for help and I had no idea how to answer them." Shuddering dramatically, she said, "It was awful. Actually, I spent most of my time wondering if I was going to see Jacob Yoder again."

"He's your new student's *daed*, right? The carpenter."

"He's Lilly's uncle. And yes, he's the carpenter." But he was also more than that. He was a man who'd given up his whole life for his family. A man who was trying his best with a grieving, confused niece.

And a man who had looked at her like she was something special.

"Hmm."

Surprised, she turned away from the turtles and glanced Lukas's way.

His lips were twitching.

"Lukas! Lukas, are you laughing at me? Are you making fun of my interest in Jacob?"

"Of course not." But his eyes were filled with humor, and he looked as if it was taking everything he had to not burst into laughter.

"Then what is so funny?"

"What isn't?" he countered. "Now you have your heart's desire and you don't like it. And in the meantime, I'm having to deal with Mercy."

She was stunned. Every time that Mercy filled in for her, Lukas acted as if she was the best substitute in the world. No, he'd acted like she was the best *replacement* in the world. In spite of herself, Rebecca had even been a bit jealous.

"Wait a minute," she blurted. "You told me you liked having her there."

He shot her a vintage Lukas look, one straight from the days when he was fifteen and acted as if he could rule the world. "Of course I was going to tell you that I liked having Mercy fill in for you. I didn't want you to stop being around *kinner* for me."

"But . . . but you aren't happy with her?"

"Oh, she's okay. She does a good job, I suppose. But when she's not hard at work? Well, she drives me crazy."

"Really?" Rebecca shouldn't have been so happy about that.

"Really," Lukas replied, his voice firm. "Becky, she's so young."

"She is eighteen."

"She's a young eighteen. She's bossy. She's chatty." He paused and glared at her. "And she flirts with half the workers."

"Oh, she does not."

"She does. Even Roman noticed and he hardly notices anything besides the pieces he works on."

If Lukas was right about that, then that said it all. Roman was the most skilled craftsman in the mill. He was given the best jobs, usually the ones where someone famous asked for a hand-carved front door or intricate woodwork around a mantel.

"It sounds as if I need to get back to my regular schedule."

"Becky, *nee*. Look, Mercy does a *gut* job. Sure she has her flaws, but we all do. If she doesn't work out, I'll hire someone else. What's important is that you find your happiness, too."

"What I'm trying to tell you is that I think my happiness might be at our family's lumber mill." When he stayed quiet, she continued. "I hadn't realized it until now, but I think I need that connection to you and Levi and our parents."

"I can understand that."

"You do?"

"Sure. That's why I'm still there, too." He smiled then and pointed to the log. "Look at your turtles, Becky."

Looking at the log, she noticed only half of them remained. "Where did they all go?"

Smiling softly, he said, "I do believe they hopped back in the water and started swimming. Some of them might even be trying to meet new, ah, male turtles."

She groaned. "Subtlety has never been your strong point, *bruder.*"

"That is true." He stretched his legs. "But it ain't been yours, either."

"So you think I should start swimming again?"

"I think you should continue to find your happiness. It's what Mamm and Daed would have wanted."

A lump filled her throat.

There was no reason to reply because she knew what he said was true. Every single word.

# Chapter 13

*Monday, September 7*

Around ten on Monday morning, Rebecca decided to have a bit of baked-good courage at Josephine's Café before she went to tell Rachel her news.

She'd just ordered a cup of coffee and a raspberry scone when she noticed Jacob Yoder had walked inside.

Taking off his hat, he glanced around and grinned when he caught her eye. "Hiya, Rebecca."

Just like that, she felt a little tremor, which she was coming to learn was her body's reaction to him. "Hi, Jacob. Coming in for breakfast?"

"*Nee*. Just a cup of coffee," he said as he walked over to her table. "My mother makes one pot of *kaffi* for us. When it's gone, it's gone. I've taken to coming in here for my third cup when I can."

"I'm having *kaffi*, too. And a scone. Want to join me?"

"I do." Motioning to Josephine, he held up his empty cup.

As he took the chair to her right, her skin tingled again. She loved how he didn't play games or act as if spending time with her was something he could take or leave. Instead, he always made her feel like she was worth his time.

"How was your weekend? Since it was our off-week for church, I didn't get to look across the way and see you and Lilly."

After thanking Josephine for his coffee and refusing her offer of a scone, he met her gaze. "It could have been better, if you want to know the truth."

"What happened?"

"Every once in a while, the reality of losing my brother and Anne hits us all hard. Sunday was one of those days. Lilly spent the majority of the day in her room. My mother went to their graves, and my father spent most of Sunday on the front porch in silence." New lines of weariness formed around his eyes as he sighed. "I didn't know what to say to anyone so I spent most of the day in the barn working on a project for Lilly."

"I'm sorry. If it's any consolation, my siblings and I have had more than a couple of days like that. They're hard ones."

"Any suggestions on how to make them easier?"

She smiled softly. "Time and prayer."

"Do you think that always helps?"

"I think so," she replied after thinking about it for a moment. "I think I had been struggling so much with the fire at the mill and our father's death, I wanted nothing more than to get away from there."

"Which is why you started volunteering at the school."

"*Jah*. But guess what happened? It turned out that helping out at the school isn't helping either me or the *kinner*! I am ill-suited to the job."

His green eyes shone with appreciation. "Surely you aren't that bad of a fit."

She giggled. "Oh, I am. Jacob, even my sister-in-law's siblings couldn't think of anything good to say about my work there . . . and they like me."

"So what are you going to do now?"

"I'm going to tell Rachel that I've decided not to help out there any longer."

"Do you think she'll be upset?"

"I can't see why she would be. I was the one who asked to volunteer. She was doing just fine without me being there. I bet she'll be relieved more than anything."

"I guess it's going to work out for almost everyone, then."

"Almost?"

He winked. "I'm going to miss Lilly's stories about you. Because of those tales, I've gotten a pretty good idea of what you've been up to."

He'd been keeping tabs on her. She was definitely not the only person who wanted to get to know the other better. "You know, if you're ever curious as to how I'm doing, you don't have to wait for Lilly to give you a report. You could stop by the lumber mill from time to time and say hello."

"You wouldn't mind?"

"*Nee*. I wouldn't mind at all."

He looked at her closely. "I'm glad we did this, Rebecca. You've made me feel better about a lot of things."

"I'm glad, though I didn't say anything noteworthy."

"You didn't? It sure felt like it. Must be the company."

Her stomach fluttered again. "Maybe so."

"You mind if I sit here a little longer? I'm starting to think I need a scone after all."

"I don't mind at all, Jacob."

RACHEL HADN'T EVER imagined that she'd want to avoid her husband, but it seemed she was better at it than she would have ever thought. She spent her morning getting ready for work, making Marcus's breakfast and lunch, then claimed she needed to get to work early for some important meetings.

Marcus hadn't looked as if he believed her for a second but he hadn't questioned her. Instead, he had gone out—either to work in the barn or leave early for work. She wasn't sure which.

As the tension between them increased, he had begun staying later and later at work. She'd taken advantage of his absence by napping the moment she got home. By the time he came home, she'd rinsed her face and put on a fresh dress. Over supper, she would chat about things that didn't matter and pretend she didn't notice when he hardly said two words.

But as they continued this pattern day after day, the strain was starting to take its toll. Marcus looked worried, and her stomach was in constant knots.

Something was going to have to change.

She was stewing about it while her students were playing outside, being supervised by two of their mothers. The women had started volunteering a bit more so Rachel could have a small break in the middle of the day.

As she slowly ate her turkey sandwich, trying to keep her nausea at bay, the door opened and Rebecca Kinsinger walked inside.

"Hi, Rachel," she said hesitantly. "I hope I'm not disturbing you?"

"Not at all. Come in and join me. I'm just finishing up my lunch." Immediately, she started to feel better. This was what she needed! A good friend to talk to. Maybe Rebecca would even want to start working more. If Rebecca took on more of each day's duties, Rachel's days would get easier. Why, she might even be able to cut her hours. Maybe then Marcus would see that her job wasn't too taxing and agree that she could work through the rest of her pregnancy.

Rebecca sat down. "I said hello to all the children outside. Three of the girls even gave me a hug."

"See, I told you that things would get easier. Children simply need time to build trust."

"I guess that's true." Rebecca smiled again, but it didn't quite reach her eyes.

Deciding to give up her attempt to eat the whole sandwich, Rachel put everything back in her insulated lunch sack. "Were you missing the *kinner*?" she asked encouragingly. "Is that why you stopped by?"

"Not exactly. I wanted to talk to you about my plans to teach."

Not wanting Rebecca to fumble through any explanations, Rachel rushed forward. "I have to say, you have perfect timing, too. I have some news for you."

"Oh?"

"I'm pregnant."

"Rachel, bless you! That's wonderful! *Wunderbaar!*" Rebecca pulled her into a quick hug. "When are you due?"

"Sometime in March."

"March! You'll be able to take your baby out to enjoy the warm spring weather."

Rachel laughed. "*Jah*, I'll have a new babe, just like all the sheep and goats around Charm." Feeling more optimistic than she had in days, Rachel smiled. "I have to say, I think you are going to be my angel," she added in a rush.

Rebecca's happy expression dimmed. "Angel?"

"You see, I haven't been feeling too *gut*, and Marcus has been concerned. I am hoping that you will want to spend even more time here."

"Oh. Well . . ."

"I'll be happy to speak with the school board and vouch for you, if you'd like. Maybe they can even start paying you for your time. After all, you'll be in here on your own when I have my baby." She held up a hand when Rebecca looked ready to argue again. "Now, don't even start to worry about whether or not you'll be ready to be on your own in the classroom. I feel certain by March you are going to be an excellent teacher, especially if you start working more and more each week."

Rebecca exhaled. "I don't think that will happen."

"Come now, think positively! Take a leap of faith! After all, we always tell the *kinner*—"

"Rachel, I'm mighty sorry, but I came here today to let you know that I won't be volunteering anymore."

"What? Why?"

"I decided that I am a better fit at the lumber mill."

Not wanting to comprehend what she was hearing, Rachel shook her head. "Is this about that day when I went to the doctor's appointment?"

"*Nee.*" She sighed. "Rachel, I haven't been enjoying myself here. Not because I don't like children or helping them . . . it's that I began to realize that being a teacher is not the job for me.

Please know that I am so grateful for your help. If it wasn't for you, I would've always had a dream that I didn't pursue. But the fact is, I don't want to be a teacher anymore."

"I see." Lifting her chin, Rachel attempted to act as if she wasn't devastated. "Well. Thank you for coming here to let me know."

Rebecca's blue eyes filled with sympathy. "I really am sorry. I had no idea that you were pregnant or that you had imagined that I might fill in for you when you had the babe."

"Of course you wouldn't have known such things. I wouldn't have expected you to read my mind. Thank you for coming to tell me in person."

"I talked to Lukas. I'm planning to go back to work full-time tomorrow. But, if you need me . . ."

"I won't need you. I will be just fine." Shaking out the skirts of her dress, she said, "Goodness! I hadn't realized how late it was! Those *kinner* are probably wondering if they're ever going to have to get back to work. And their mothers are no doubt wondering the same thing."

Looking concerned, Rebecca nodded. "*Jah*. I had better go so you can get back to work. Thank you again for everything and . . . well, Rachel, I hope this won't hurt our friendship."

"Of course it won't," she said in a rush before turning away. Her head was spinning and she was so disappointed by Rebecca's change of heart, she could hardly look at her. Instead, she opened the door and stepped into the bright sunlight.

Thankfully, no one seemed to have noticed that her lunch had gone on for ten minutes too long. All the *kinner* were either playing four square, chatting with the mothers, or talking to one another on the picnic table.

"Scholars, it's time to line up!" she called out as Rebecca walked down the steps.

Immediately, the children started forward with a burst of excited chatter. Rebecca slipped out through the middle of the crowd. The children hardly acknowledged her. Instead, nearly every one of Rachel's thirty students was staring up at her with a look of expectation.

And trust.

That simple gesture eased Rachel like little else. She didn't know what was going to happen to her classroom or with her and Marcus. All she knew was that she didn't regret choosing to teach as long as she possibly could. She loved these *kinner*. She loved this job, and she felt as if the Lord had given her the temperament and knowledge to do it well.

Somehow, some way, she was simply going to have to get her husband to understand that. No, what she needed to do was take a page from Rebecca's book. She needed to find a way to follow her own dreams, even when that was hard to do.

As much as she wanted Marcus to be happy, she wanted to be happy, too. After all, she had a wee baby to think of.

# Chapter 14

*Tuesday, September 8*

After breaking the news to Rachel and the energizing conversation she'd shared with Jacob, Rebecca had delved into household chores so she could go back to work feeling like she'd helped Amelia as much as she could.

She'd spent the majority of yesterday helping Amelia with laundry and turning the last of the tomato crop into spaghetti sauce. By the time Darla joined them at five and Lukas came home at six, all the sheets had been removed from the line outside, been neatly folded, and put away into the linen closet. There were also a dozen jars of sauce on the kitchen counter ready to be stored in the cellar.

For a brief moment, Rebecca had wondered if she'd been too hasty in deciding that teaching wasn't for her. But when she realized that doubt came from wanting to help Rachel through her pregnancy, not spend all her days in the Amish schoolhouse, she'd known she made the right decision.

Now, at last, Rebecca felt like she'd made peace with her decision. Perhaps there really was no shame in coming to terms with the fact that some dreams were not meant to ever be realized.

Because of that, she'd felt more than ready to head back to the reception area at the mill this morning. Her body had felt refreshed and her mood had been lifted. Renewed. She was eager to tackle whatever came her way.

"It's mighty *gut* to have you back, Rebecca," Simon Hochstetler announced as he strode inside the main building. "I was beginning to miss your bossy ways."

"You say the nicest things," she teased. "I don't know what I did without you men making me feel so *gut* about myself."

"Prepare yourself," he said with a wink. "If you stick around, you might hear even more compliments."

She knew his silly quip wasn't quite as lighthearted as it sounded. Things hadn't been running as smoothly in her absence as she'd been led to believe.

When Simon rested his arms on the marble countertop in front of her, she smiled at him expectantly. "What can I do for ya?"

His lips twitched. "Look a little farther to the left, Rebecca. What do you see?"

When she did as he bid, she gasped. Two unexpected items were on the counter. One was a white takeout cup filled with coffee and the other was a small paper bag. Both were emblazoned with the word HOLTZMAN's in bold blue letters.

She got to her feet. "You brought me Holtzman *kaffi* and donuts?"

He smiled, no doubt catching the thread of wonder in her voice. "I did. And they are your favorites, too. I brought you a buttermilk cake donut."

"Bless you." He was right. Buttermilk cake was her favorite.

"Inside the cup is Holtzman's dark *kaffi* blend. I added just a hint of cream, too."

Unable to wait another second, she pulled off the plastic top and took a tentative sip. Then another one. It was beyond delicious. A third sip led her to see that it was, indeed, prepared exactly the way she liked it. She almost moaned. It was really that good.

"*Danke*, Simon. This was the perfect welcome-back gift. It was so kind of you. So thoughtful. Really, thank you. I don't know what to say."

He shrugged. "It's just *kaffi* and a donut, Becky. A simple thank-you is more than enough."

Not caring that it would be better manners to wait until he went back to work to eat her donut, she pulled out her treat and took a bite.

Looking extremely pleased by her reaction, he said, "Does it taste as good as you had hoped?"

"Even better. You're wonderful."

He laughed. "That's quite the compliment. Now I know what to do in the future if I need to soften you up."

"*Jah*, this will do it." She took another bite, enjoying the cake's crunchy exterior and sweet buttermilk goodness. After another sip of coffee, she set both down and pushed them to one side. "All right, Simon. Tell me what you need and I'll see if I can do it. What happened? Did you mess up an order again? Or do you need me to make some phone calls for you?" Simon hated to talk on the phone.

"*Nee*. It, ah, it ain't nothing like that," he mumbled as he glanced covertly behind him. Directly at Lukas's closed office door.

At first Rebecca thought he was hoping to see Lukas. But closer inspection made her realize that he wasn't looking for her brother. Instead, it seemed Simon was actually hoping *not* to see him.

"Is something wrong? Is someone on your team giving you trouble?" she asked.

Every worker at Kinsinger Lumber Mill was part of a team. From time to time, disputes erupted. When that happened, most people simply went to Lukas for help. But every once in a while men came to her for advice. She was close enough to Lukas to know what was going on, but talking to her held none of the stigma of complaining to the boss.

His brows snapped together in confusion, then he shook his head. "*Nee*. It's not that at all."

"What is it?"

"Well, I want to do something, but I'm going to need your help."

She'd known him for most of her life and had rarely seen him look so serious or hesitant. Simon was outgoing. Simon was blunt. He did not beat around the bush.

"What do you need my help with?"

After glancing toward Lukas's closed office door again, he said, "Amelia."

Amelia? As in her little sister? "I'm afraid I'm not following you," she said slowly. Because she was really, really hoping he wasn't about to say what she feared.

He stepped back from her desk, his arms at his sides. "Rebecca, it's like this. I want to see her."

Pure discomfort settled deep inside her. "You know where she lives," she said, hoping he'd take her statement as a joke.

He didn't. Instead, he scowled. "Rebecca, you know what I mean. I want to court Amelia."

"*Nee.*" She shook her head for added emphasis.

Simon—much to Rebecca's dismay—didn't look surprised about her knee-jerk reaction. "Listen. She's more than old enough. I've been biding my time, but I canna wait anymore to make a move."

"She is old enough, but Amelia is tenderhearted."

"I know that."

"She's also far younger than you."

Looking irritated, he snapped, "She's six years younger. Not twenty."

"That's still a bit of a gap," she protested, trying her best to forget that Jacob Yoder was thirty years to her twenty-five.

"I know that, too. However, we have all known each other forever, Becky. You can't be surprised."

She didn't want to hurt his feelings, but she didn't want to encourage him, either. "Since we have known each other for so long, you and I both know what you're asking ain't a *gut* idea. At all."

He folded his arms over his chest. "I don't see why you would say that. I've been your brother's best friend for most of our lives. I work for your family's company."

Everything he said was true. But none of that mattered when it came to protecting her sister's heart. "This is different, though." Why, *why* had he come to her instead of Lukas?

His tone turned hard. "Why is me wanting to court Amelia any different? She's a beautiful girl, Rebecca. Sweet as can be. I'll treat her well. You know I will."

That was the problem. She knew Simon would treasure Amelia. But no amount of care would ever change the fact that he was not suitable for her. Simon was from a troubled home. It was no secret that things had been bad enough there for him to leave when he was fourteen or fifteen.

Furthermore, she'd heard more than a couple of disturbing rumors highlighting his activities once he'd moved out. When he returned to Charm at eighteen, he'd gone directly to her father and had a private meeting with him. When he left, it had been with both an entry-level job at the mill and, she suspected, enough money to lease a small apartment. Her father had never talked about their conversation, but he had trusted Simon enough to offer him employment.

Still, Rebecca was fairly sure that he would have had someone far different in mind to be Amelia's beau. Someone from a secure family. Someone who didn't have a secret past or all sorts of rumors swirling around him.

Ack, but she wished things could have simply stayed the same!

At the very least, she wished that he would have approached her brother instead. "I wish you would have gone to Lukas about this."

He rolled his eyes. "Why? So Lukas could tell me no before I even had a chance to explain myself?" Staring at her intently, he said, "Rebecca, I need you to give me a chance. I know Amelia wants me to court her. I *know* it. But she ain't going to go against Lukas, not after losing your *daed*."

"Amelia is still grieving our father. She might not be ready to think about courting."

"Just like you aren't?"

Immediately, she thought of Jacob Yoder. Would she turn him away if he approached her? After the warm connection she'd felt at Josephine's, she knew she wouldn't.

But that was different, wasn't it?

"Amelia is far more tenderhearted than I am. With Mamm gone, I need to look out for her."

"You aren't. Your interference is only going to cause her harm. I don't want her to start doubting herself or doubting my regard for her. I need to call on her properly." Sounding even more frustrated, he added, "You have to know how awkward this is for me, Becky. I'm a grown man asking permission to call on a grown woman. You need to respect that."

"I do." She stopped herself before saying anything unkind. "I like you, Simon. But you and I both know that you would not be a good match for someone as sheltered as my little sister."

"You're serious, aren't you?"

"I'm afraid so." Seeing the pain in his eyes, she winced. However, she knew she was doing the right thing. All of them— Lukas, Levi, even their parents—had wanted the best for Amelia. As much as it pained her to admit it, it wasn't Simon.

Now feeling more sure of herself, she said, "Simon, with our parents now gone and Levi off doing who-knows-what, it's up to me and Lukas to look after Amelia. She was little more than a child when our *mamm* passed. In many ways, I raised her."

"I understand that. But we both know that I am not going to treat her badly. I am not going to take her for granted. I want to look after her, too. You know she would be happy with me."

Even thinking about Amelia in Simon's care made Rebecca uncomfortable. "I'm sorry, Simon, but I don't agree."

"Don't say that."

Seeking to end the conversation without making things even worse, she ignored his harsh tone and angry expression. "Listen, don't worry about Lukas. I won't say anything to him."

"No, feel free to share. I can't wait to hear what he says."

She hated hurting him, but she needed to do the right thing, even if it made things between them uncomfortable. "I appreciate you coming to talk to me, and the donut and coffee, too. But my mind is made up. I don't want you courting her. Ever."

"Ever," he echoed. His voice was bleak. "Can I ask what exactly I've done that makes me so unsuitable?"

"You know what you've done."

He shook his head. "Don't be vague. You owe me more than that."

She really didn't want to answer him. However, his expression was hard. So different than she'd ever seen it. She owed him an explanation. "I heard rumors about your *rumspringa,* Simon. And what happened to you."

He flinched.

Thinking about the whispered comments and veiled references made her stomach feel like it had a cold knot sitting in the middle of it. She imagined that some of what was said about his "running around time" was exaggerated. But not all of it could have been made up. Like her father used to say, where there was smoke there was fire. "Don't make me say any more."

"No, you don't have to say a single thing more," he said, just as Lukas's office door opened. Simon walked out the front door as Lukas entered the reception area.

With a sinking heart, she watched Simon turn left, no doubt taking the long way back to one of the older warehouses on the property. She'd just made an enemy out of him, or at the very least, she'd lost his friendship.

Now she was going to have to figure out what to tell Lukas. As much as she had hoped to keep him out of it, she feared that he was going to notice the new animosity looming between her and Simon.

But when?

The clearing of a throat knocked her back into the present. She blinked, then blinked again as she took in who was approaching her circular reception desk. Lukas—with Jacob Yoder by his side. Had she been so fixated on Simon that she hadn't even noticed Jacob enter the offices?

"Hi, Jacob," she said.

"Hey. Are you okay?"

She was still pretty rattled from her exchange with Simon, but she sure wasn't going to tell him about that. "I'll be fine. I just, um, had a difficult conversation with someone."

While Jacob continued to watch her, Lukas glanced out the window. "What kind of difficult conversation? And why did Simon just leave out the front door?"

"I'm not sure."

Lukas's brow wrinkled. "Huh. Well, what was he doing here? Is there a problem?"

"I don't think there are any problems that you need to know about." She held up the takeout cup, which didn't seem nearly as inviting as it had just minutes before. "Simon just stopped by to bring me coffee and a donut."

Lukas raised his eyebrows. "From Holtzman's. Wow, I'm impressed. What did he want?"

Rebecca would have smiled if she wasn't so upset. "Oh, um, nothing." When Lukas's eyes narrowed, she blurted, "He just, um, wanted me to help him with a couple of phone calls. You know how he hates those." Turning back to Jacob, she attempted to laugh. "That was our friend Simon Hochstetler. He's a capable man and one of our best managers. He ain't too good when it comes to talking on the phone, however."

"It's good you're here then," Jacob said. His tone was steady, but it was completely obvious that he knew she was hiding something.

Feeling warm, she smiled at him softly.

Lukas's bark of laughter interrupted the moment. "*Jah*. He hates talking on the phone more than anyone I've ever met. Will you handle his calls?"

"Of course I will. You know I'll help Simon with anything I can." With effort, she kept her expression easy and open. It was difficult, though, because she hated lying.

"*Gut. Danke.*"

"Thanks ain't necessary." Remembering what she'd offered Jacob, her cheeks flamed. "So, did you decide to visit the mill?"

"I would have, but after our conversation, I decided to do a little soul-searching, too. I came in for a job."

"A job here?" She looked from Jacob to Lukas in confusion. "I thought you were farming your parents' land."

"*Jah*. Well, like your teaching job, farming wasn't really a good fit for me."

Lukas grinned. "*Jah*. It seems that there's more than one person in Charm who is searching for the right occupation."

Knowing he was teasing, she raised her chin and tried to look full of herself. "Discovering the right path for one's future ain't all that easy, Lukas."

Jacob grinned. "Oh, let him tease ya, Rebecca. The way I see it, I'm in pretty good company."

His gentle flirting made her insides flutter. Afraid she was about to either say something silly or turn bright crimson, she picked up one of the many pencils on her desk and started fiddling with it.

Lukas said, "Jake here has even more experience than I realized. I just hired him. He's going to work over in the far warehouse, building frames for Millers Builders." Handing Rebecca a blue file folder, he added, "All the papers that he needs to fill out are inside. After he completes them, will you get him processed? He'll start next Monday."

"Of course I will," she replied as Lukas walked away. When they were alone, Rebecca smiled at Jacob. "Welcome to the Kinsinger family. I hope you will enjoy working here."

He smiled back. "*Danke*, Rebecca. I'm glad to be here."

She realized right then that she was glad he was there, too. She just wished his arrival hadn't come on the heels of rejecting Simon's request to court Amelia.

There was something very difficult about welcoming a man like Jacob into her life while putting up roadblocks for another man who had been nothing but kind to her for as long as she could remember.

# Chapter 15

The way Rebecca was looking at him made Jacob realize that he'd made the right decision. No matter how hard it had been to accept that he wasn't ever going to be able to take his brother's place and farm the land, it seemed the Lord was in complete agreement. How else could Jacob explain that Rebecca's sweet smile had been the first thing he'd encountered after accepting Lukas's generous job offer? He needed no other sign that he was doing the right thing.

Realizing he was staring at Rebecca foolishly, he clasped the folder Lukas had left on the counter. "It is *gut* to see ya. I trust you are still doing well?"

She tilted her head to one side and smiled softly. "I am. It looks like you are, too."

"I am, indeed. Our little talk yesterday really helped. Thanks, again."

"After talking with you I felt better, too."

He loved how easily she blushed around him. He lifted up the file folder. "So, would you like me to read through all the paperwork and bring it back to you?"

She was still gazing at him like she had a secret. "Well, you could do that, Jacob," she said slowly. "But if you have the time, you could simply fill it out here. That way I'll be able to enter all your information in the computer. I can give you a key and a time card, too. And maybe even take you on a tour of the property, if you want one."

He wanted one. Well, he wanted to spend more time with her. "You have time for that?"

"Today I do." She ran a hand over the surface of a desktop that looked freshly polished.

"I guess that means you talked to Mrs. Mast."

"I did. After we talked, I finally got up my nerve and told Rachel that I wasna going to be able to continue to help her out anymore."

"I wondered if you did." Noticing that she looked uneasy, he said, "So, how did she take it?"

"I'd be lying if I said she looked happy about my news, but it seemed to go well enough."

"Based on what Lilly's told me, I think Mrs. Mast really cares about her students. Once she realizes that you weren't the best fit for her class, she'll come around." Hoping to be encouraging, he brightened his tone. "I bet she already has."

"I really hope so." She bit her lip as a new shadow entered her expression. "She and I have been friends for a long time. It's hard telling a friend something they don't want to hear, you know?"

"I know. It's because you don't want to disappoint them."

"*Jah*. Exactly." The dimple popped in her check. "Anyway, now I am just going to be working here."

That didn't sound like a bad thing at all. "So we'll be seeing each other all the time."

She chuckled. "It would seem so."

Jacob had a feeling that there was far more to that story, but it sure wasn't his place to prod her for more information. Instead, he picked up the folder, grabbed a pen from the container on her desk, and walked over to a nearby chair. After grabbing a magazine to use as a makeshift desk, he began completing the forms.

"Let me know if you have any questions about the papers," Rebecca said as she straightened a stack of folders that didn't look like they needed straightening at all.

"I will, though none of it looks difficult." Most of it was basic information: his address, contact information, and payment options. There were also questions about his transportation needs. Kinsinger offered van service to Amish workers in the morning and evening. He checked that he would need to be picked up and dropped off.

When he was almost done, he glanced at Rebecca. To his surprise, she was staring at him. Curious, he smiled at her.

She blinked, and immediately looked away.

Not wanting to embarrass her, he stared at one of the forms. But instead of carefully filling it out, his mind drifted back to Rebecca. What was she thinking?

Had she been staring at him?

And the way she'd averted her eyes? Well, it was almost like a shy schoolgirl around a crush. At least, that was how he remembered girls acting back when he'd been at school in Pinecraft.

Could it be that she felt the same attraction for him that he felt for her?

Ten minutes later, he finished everything and brought it to her. "Here you go."

"*Danke.*" Not quite meeting his eyes, she took it. "Now I just need to enter everything in the computer. It will take about fifteen minutes or so."

"I've got time."

"I can do that for ya, Becky," a petite young woman said brightly as she strode forward.

Rebecca turned to the girl. "It's new employee information. You're going to need to start a file for Jacob. Have you ever done that before?"

"I have." The girl smiled at Jacob. "Are you a new employee?"

"I am. My name's Jacob Yoder."

"Hiya. I'm Mercy Graber." Her bright smile widened, showing a little gap between her two front teeth. "I'm kind of new, too. I've only been working at Kinsinger's for six months. And only at the reception desk for a couple of weeks."

"She's already doing a *gut* job, though," Rebecca said as she stood up. "How about I take you on that tour now?"

"Sounds *gut*."

Mercy looked at him and Rebecca with a puzzled frown. "Oh, do you want me to do the tour? It's no—"

"*Nee.* I want you to input the paperwork," Rebecca said firmly. "I will take Jacob around."

"Oh!" Looking a little sheepish, Mercy smiled again. "All right. I understand now."

Jacob could have sworn he heard Rebecca groan as she walked around her workstation. He did his best to keep his expression blank, though it was tempting to grin.

"Let's start in the back and work our way forward," she said.

He waved a hand. "Lead and I'll follow."

Looking a bit flustered, Rebecca strode forward, opened the front door, and motioned for him to join her.

When the door closed behind them, and Rebecca was practically marching toward the back of the property, Jacob spoke. "Do you not care for Mercy?"

"What? Oh, I like her fine."

"Ah."

Her steps slowed. "I guess I couldn't have been more obvious, huh? She's a good worker and tries hard. I just sometimes feel like I need to make it clear that she helps me, not the other way around."

"I can understand that. That happened from time to time when I was working on jobs in Sarasota. Some men wanted to be in charge all the time, even when they didn't know what they were doing."

She grinned. "Exactly. Mercy's enthusiasm sometimes needs to be tempered a bit. Or it might be a case of me needing to be more patient with her." Turning, she said, "This here is the main gate, where all the big trucks load and unload shipments."

He was impressed. "It's a big place. I didn't realize Kinsinger's covered so much property."

"Before we asked all workers, both Amish and English, to get on email, we used to hire teenagers to run messages around. Those boys were constantly on the run. It's a big property with almost two hundred employees."

"Quite a legacy to take care of."

"I suppose it is," she said. "Funny, I never thought of the company like that. In fact, I usually considered it a burden because my father spent more hours here than he did at home." She closed her eyes, hating how selfish that made her sound. The mill had supported her family for years.

"Is that why you were working at the school?"

"*Jah.*" She looked at him out of the corner of her eye, then said, "I was trying to find my place. It's funny, but once Lukas pretty much assured me that I could leave and even got Mercy to fill in, I started realizing that I didn't want to leave my job as much as I thought I did." After a moment, she rolled her eyes. "I also have to tell ya that those *kinner* scared me half to death."

"Scared you?" Now, that caught him off guard. She seemed like a pretty confident woman. Her brother had also told him that she handled a lot of things at the company. Even though she'd said that she hadn't enjoyed her time at the Amish school, Jacob would have never thought that she would use a descriptor like that. "Most of those *kinner* weren't very big, Rebecca," he teased.

"It wasn't their height that scared me, it was how demanding they were. Plus, I didn't always feel like I could help them." Lowering her voice, she added, "That's what scared me the most. I hated that."

"I feel that way with Lilly."

"Rachel told me that Lilly is going to need some special instruction because she's so bright. Does that worry you?"

It felt good to talk about his insecurities. "Not at all," he said after a moment. "I simply want her to be happy. To be frank, I'm kind of glad that she has something else to focus on. Those first few weeks after her parents died were so hard on her."

"I can imagine." Her voice sounded a little melancholy.

Jacob wondered if she was referring to her father's death. But before he could think of something suitable to say, she seemed to realize that they were standing motionless in the middle of the loading bay, and started walking again.

"I'll take you into each building," she said over her shoulder. "But don't feel like you need to learn your way around. The men on your team will show you what to do and where to go on Monday."

"Whatever you want to do is fine."

She led him into a large warehouse. "This is where you will probably be working. It's where most of the carpenters work. We also keep all the special-order pieces of lumber here."

"Special order?" He loved listening to her speak about Kinsinger Lumber. She might not realize it, but there was a lot of pride in her voice whenever she talked about her family's company.

"Like big slabs of redwood from the West Coast."

Rebecca led the way around, exchanging greetings with most of the men in the warehouse. Every so often, she would stop and introduce him or explain a certain machine.

Jacob was impressed. Not just about the facility but how knowledgeable she was about pretty much every facet of the company. As they exited one building and entered another, his appreciation for her grew. He especially liked how she interacted with all the employees. Whether they were older men or boys in their late teens, she knew everyone's name and something about them. All the men treated her as if she were a sister. They joked with her and answered her questions.

Jacob also liked that she didn't seem especially close to any of them.

When they entered the main building and she showed him around the retail store, Jacob found himself wondering more and more about her personal relationships and far less about break rooms or employees' names. By the time she asked if he'd like to join her for a glass of iced tea at the small café on the top floor, Jacob knew he wanted to know a whole lot more about her.

"I happened to notice that you are *gut* friends with a lot of the men here."

"We've all worked together for some time. Some men are second- and even third-generation employees, just like Lukas and myself. We've all grown up together."

"So you're close to them."

*"Jah."* She looked at him curiously. "What are you getting at?"

"I'm trying to figure out if you are seeing any of the men." Because she looked confused, he decided to be completely blunt. "Like, in a romantic way."

Her eyebrows shot straight up. "Of course not."

"Why, of course not?"

"Jacob, I don't date employees." She sounded incredulous that he would even think such a thing.

"Ever?" he clarified.

"I haven't yet." She smiled then.

He knew a flirtatious smile when he saw one. Feeling bolder, he asked, "What about someone new? Like, say, a man who was new to Charm. A new employee who is, you know, attempting to make friends."

Her blue eyes sparkled. "Well. Hmm. It would be awful of me to ignore an offer of friendship."

"Is it against the company rules for employees to see each other?"

*"Nee."* After taking what seemed like a fortifying breath, she said, "Actually, some of our men are married to the women who work in the café or retail store."

"So, even though you never have spent time with any of the men who work here . . . you might? If the person was right?"

Her cheeks and neck turned pink. "Jacob, are you . . . are you asking me out?"

"I'd like to. If I asked you, what do you think you might say?"

She bit her bottom lip. "I'd probably warn you that I'm kind of a handful. Things in my family are a little scattered, too. You know about my *daed* recently passing."

Taking care to speak softly so that she'd understand he was being completely serious, he replied, "I know. And I even heard the rumors about your brother leaving."

"Because of all that, I don't really have a lot of extra time."

"I don't need a lot of your time. Just some of it."

Her eyes widened. She sipped her tea, then she straightened her shoulders. "I canna believe I'm saying this, but okay."

"Okay?"

When she nodded, a surprised look on her face, he grinned at her. "That makes me mighty happy." She smiled weakly back, and Jacob decided that he had better push a little bit before she started overthinking things and changed her mind. "So, when do you get off work today?"

"At four o'clock." Her voice was still hesitant. It was cute.

"So, may I walk you home?"

"*Jah*. But I live close by. How will you get home after that?"

"I can walk there."

She crossed her legs and chuckled softly. "You're not wasting any time, are you?"

"I'm afraid if I give you too much time to think about it, you might change your mind and tell me no after all," he said honestly.

"You might be as ruthlessly honest as I have a tendency to be. Come to my desk when I get off. I'll be waiting."

"I'll be there," he said as they walked down the stairs to her desk. After getting his key and folder from Mercy, he walked outside.

He had some time to kill. Then he was going to do something he'd never expected to do when he'd packed up his things and moved to Charm.

He was going courting.

Just the idea of it made him grin.

# Chapter 16

*That same day*

It was turning out to be quite the Tuesday for Lilly Yoder. First, Mrs. Mast had asked her to stay a few minutes after school to talk. Then, when she'd told Peter that she couldn't walk home with him after all, he'd offered to stay behind and wait for her. Right in front of his best friend Andy, Katie, and another handful of people. Lilly, of course, had blushed like crazy. Because that was all she seemed able to do around Peter. But that didn't stop her from telling him thank you.

Beyond all of that, Katie was talking to her again. At first, she'd only said hello and talked about her little brother's new rabbit. When she'd realized Lilly wasn't going to hold a grudge, Katie sat next to her at lunch.

"You don't mind if I sit with ya, do you?" she'd asked.

"Why would I mind?" After all, it wasn't like she had that many friends.

"Probably because I haven't been that nice to you lately."

"What did I do?"

Katie chomped on a carrot stick. "It weren't that as much as what Peter did. He's been following you around like a puppy." Around another bite, she said, "I was pretty jealous."

Lilly wasn't sure what Katie could be jealous of—she was the one who had all the friends. Then she remembered the way Katie had glared at her when Peter was talking to her the other day. "I'm sorry. I didn't know you and Peter were seeing each other."

"We weren't."

So Katie had been holding on to a crush? "Oh. Well, I guess I should tell you that it wasn't anything personal. I honestly didn't try to get Peter to start walking me home. It just happened."

To Lilly's amusement, Katie shrugged off her concerns as if they were of no consequence at all. "Don't worry about it. I was being foolish. The truth is that Peter and I have known each other all our lives. We've never been all that close or even that good of friends. I don't know why I thought he'd one day start looking at me in a new way."

"Oh. I see." Of course, Lilly really didn't, but if things were fine between them now, she wasn't going to argue.

Sighing dramatically, Katie added, "Actually, last night I was thinking about why I was so upset with you. And that's when I realized something."

"What?"

"See, I wasn't only jealous of Peter liking you. I was jealous of you, too."

Her? "Katie, you're the one with all the friends. What are you talking about?"

"You're pretty, Lilly. And smart, too. And it's even kind of nice that you are new here. All the kids might like me now, but they remember when I couldn't say my 'R's and used to suck my thumb."

Lilly burst out laughing. "You are pretty, too. And I haven't noticed you slip up with your 'R's yet."

Katie chuckled, too. "*Gut*. What I'm trying to say is that you being here reminded me of everything I'm not and it made me kind of sad. I'm sorry."

"It's okay."

"*Danke.*" With another smile, Katie had dived into her sandwich and started telling Lilly another story about her many siblings. They sounded like a wild bunch. One of them was always getting hurt or injured or in trouble.

Lilly had been happy to simply listen and eat her sandwich. As she did so, she realized that Katie hadn't brought up Lilly's parents dying once. Maybe Peter had glared at her so much the other day that she was afraid to mention Lilly's parents ever again.

But Lilly preferred to think that Katie had started thinking of Lilly as just, well, Lilly. The new girl. Not Lilly, the poor girl whose parents died and who had to live with her grandparents and uncle.

If that was the case, she would be thankful for that.

Late that afternoon, when Mrs. Mast reentered the classroom after dismissing school for the day, Peter was following her.

"It's pretty warm outside. I didn't have the heart to make Peter stand in the sun while waiting for you," Mrs. Mast explained. "Do you mind if he sits in the back of the classroom while you and I chat near my desk?"

After casting a quick glance in Peter's direction and seeing him shrug, Lilly shrugged, too. "Sure. That's fine."

"Good," she said as she walked to her desk. "Now then, I bet you know why I wanted to speak to you."

"Is it because I was working on algebra in your classroom?"

"It is."

"I won't do that again."

"Lilly, you certainly aren't in trouble. Actually, I went over to the high school the other day and talked to some of my teacher friends there."

This was starting to sound bad. "What did they say?" she asked hesitantly. Oh, she really hoped no one wanted her to start attending the English high school.

Mrs. Mast's kind eyes softened. "My friend Blaire wants you to go over there on Monday. She's going to meet you at the door and—"

"*Nee*," Lilly interrupted. "I don't want to go to the high school."

Mrs. Mast held up a hand. "No one wants you to transfer over there. All Blaire wants to do is give you some tests."

"Why?"

"If you score as high as I think you might, Blaire is going to help me gather some materials for you." She paused, then added, "And find you some tutors."

"Could I do the work here?" Though she hadn't meant to, she glanced over at Peter.

He'd moved closer and was making no secret that he was eavesdropping on the conversation. When she looked his way, he smiled. That smile helped enough to make her stop questioning everything her teacher was saying.

"I'm sorry. I'll stop interrupting so much."

Mrs. Mast grinned, then looked over her shoulder. "Peter,

since it's obvious that you're listening, and since I have no doubt that you and Lilly will talk about this the whole way home, you might as well join the conversation."

"*Danke*, Aunt Rachel," he said, walking right over and, bold-as-you-please, sitting on Lilly's other side.

Unable to help herself, Lilly giggled. "You are incorrigible, Peter."

"Since I'm not even sure what that means, I think you need to go to the high school on Monday and meet Blaire and get tested," he replied.

"Who would the tutors be?" Lilly asked. "And where would I meet them?"

"They are going to be high school juniors and seniors who can drive. They'll come here once or twice a week and help you understand everything you're working on."

"So I would still be here, but I'd be working on my own a lot."

"*Jah.*" Mrs. Mast's expression was somber. "Lilly, my job as a teacher is to help my students. If I thought you needed glasses, I would help you get to the eye doctor. If you were having a lot of trouble learning and I feared that you needed a special class or teacher, I would do that, too. As far as I'm concerned, your needs are no less important than anyone else's. They're simply a bit unusual."

Lilly liked that statement. Plus, it would be so nice to learn something new instead of always pretending to be interested in what everyone else was trying to figure out.

But still . . . What would her grandparents say?

"Would the tutors be expensive?" she asked.

"They wouldn't be expensive at all. They would be free," Mrs. Mast explained.

"Oh."

"When would she go over to the high school?" Peter asked.

"Blaire said she could drive over here and pick you up during her morning break. So you'd go to the high school a little after nine, then either Blaire or another teacher would drive you back here."

"I'll still need to talk with my uncle Jacob and my grandparents."

"I understand. Just let me know by the end of the week. If you decide you don't want help, when Blaire stops by, I'll tell her that you changed your mind," Mrs. Mast said easily.

"All right, then. I guess I'll let you know on Thursday or Friday."

"I'm proud of you, Lilly," Mrs. Mast said as she stood up and walked her and Peter to the door. "I know you've been through a lot and that this is another change. But I think you'll be really glad you decided to do this."

"*Danke*," Lilly said. "You went to a lot of trouble for me. It was mighty nice of you."

"You're welcome, dear." Stepping back, Mrs. Mast said, "Now you two go enjoy your evening."

"We sure will, Aunt Rachel," Peter said. "See you tomorrow."

"*Jah*. I'll see you then." Wagging a finger at him playfully, she added, "But don't you forget to do your homework."

His grin slipped away. "I won't."

"*Gut*." After winking Lilly's way, Mrs. Mast closed the door behind them.

When they were alone, Peter laughed. "I think she's said that to me every afternoon for five years."

"I guess there was a reason for that?"

"*Jah*. I got pretty lazy when I was eight or nine. Our former teacher had to ask my parents to help keep me in line. They warned me to be better behaved for Aunt Rachel when she started here."

"Did you listen?"

He rubbed his rear end. "Oh, *jah*. My *daed* made sure of it."

"Ouch."

He shrugged off her sympathy. "It weren't so bad. Like I said, I've always been kind of a handful."

"You've been really nice to me," she said as they crossed the stretch of empty highway, then detoured onto a narrow path that lay between two different farms. Everyone walked down it to get from one end of Charm to the other.

So far, Lilly had only been on it when most of the other kids were there. Now it was just the two of them.

It felt different.

Peter glanced her way and grinned again. "Of course I'm going to be nice to you."

"Why?"

He stared straight ahead. "You know why," he said after a good five minutes.

She really didn't. Her worst fears got the best of her. "Is it because my parents died?"

He stopped suddenly. "*Nee.*"

Now she was really confused. Glancing around, she felt like they were the only two people for miles around. There was a faint breeze making the hay in the field on their left rustle in the wind.

"Then why?" she asked.

He sighed, looked at her backpack on her shoulder, then

reached out and set it on the ground. He tossed his down with a lot less care. While she stood there gaping at him, he took both of her hands in his. It was the first time she'd ever held a boy's hand. She noticed his hands were far bigger and rougher.

"Peter?"

"I like you, Lilly," he said at last. "I think you're pretty. I like how you're kind of shy. I like how you're really smart. I like how you put up with Katie and her goofy ways. But what I like the most is that you are letting me walk you home."

"I'm letting you hold my hands, too," she pointed out.

He squeezed her hands gently. "*Jah*. Today? Well, today's a really *gut* day." He dropped her hands then and picked up their backpacks. "Now, do you have any more questions, Miss I'm-too-smart-for-regular-school?"

She couldn't help it, she burst out laughing just as she grabbed her backpack from him and started walking. When he chuckled too as he fell into step beside her, she knew Peter had been right. It surely was a really good day.

# Chapter 17

*That same day*

It was a beautiful early September afternoon. Though the air was warm, the humidity had lessened. A slight breeze filled the air, bringing with it a hint of the upcoming change in season. Those elements, combined with the many terra-cotta pots of dark red geraniums, yellow mums, and pretty purple pansies, made walking outside a pleasure.

But Rebecca was beginning to think that the main reason the day felt so perfect was because Jacob was by her side.

He'd returned to the office at four o'clock on the dot. Then, he'd stood patiently by the door as she cleared off her desk and gathered her purse and keys. Of course that had taken double the time it usually did, what with her smiling at him, losing her train of thought, and generally behaving like a schoolgirl instead of the independent working woman that she was.

When she'd finally announced that she was ready to go, he'd smiled.

"I'm glad," he'd said. As if nothing else was needed to be said. And maybe nothing else did.

His easy acceptance of her made her feel special, which was a mighty nice feeling.

Now, as they continued to walk, she noticed that Jacob was measuring his steps to hers. It was a kind thing to do. So many men would have expected her to walk faster to keep their pace. His accommodation was a sign, she thought. A sign that they were supposed to enjoy this time together as much as possible. And, perhaps, use it to discover more about each other.

"Hey, Jacob?"

"*Jah?*"

"Do you remember when I was walking home with Lilly? We were on that path in between the Hendrix and Montgomery properties and had almost made it to town?"

"If you are asking if I remember overhearing Lilly being terribly rude to you, the answer is yes. I remember that well."

Rebecca noticed that his voice had darkened. She also sensed that he was about to apologize to her again. She decided to get to her point, and quickly.

"Well, before all that, Lilly asked me a funny question."

Looking down at her, Jacob grimaced. "Do I even want to know? Half the things that I hear come out of her mouth are surprising."

"Don't sound so glum," she said pertly. "First of all, girls her age are dramatic."

"I believe that."

He sounded so confused about it that Rebecca laughed. "Being dramatic is not a bad thing. I promise!"

"All right. If you say so." He sighed. "I tell you what, I am looking forward to the day when Lilly and I are more comfortable with each other. I hope and pray that one day I can tell her something without feeling like I am walking on eggshells."

Boy, she'd started this off on a bad foot. "Jacob, I didn't bring this up to talk about Lilly." Before she started blushing, she cleared her throat. "Lilly asked if I had ever had a boyfriend."

"I'm sorry. That girl has no shame." He shook his head. "How did you answer that? Or do I even want to know?"

She smiled in return, liking both his joke and his honesty. "Well, you see, that caught me off guard. I actually thought it was kind of a funny question."

"Of course you did. It weren't any of her business."

"No, it was actually because I hadn't really reflected on my past relationships—or lack of them. You see, my answer was no. I've never had a serious boyfriend."

"There's nothing wrong with that."

"I don't think so, either. But when she then asked me why I hadn't, I got to thinking some more." After a brief pause, she continued on. It was obvious that she needed to get to the point soon, before he began thinking she was being critical of his niece.

"When I was attempting to give her reasons as to why I hadn't ever had a boyfriend, I discovered something about myself."

"What was that?"

"I never gave myself the time or opportunity to do so."

"Truly?" He sounded surprised.

She didn't blame him. She'd been kind of surprised about her romance-less state, too. "I started thinking about my life. At first I decided I could say that I've simply been too busy for love and romance. But once I was honest with myself, I realized that I've actually let myself become too busy. I allowed myself to put other people's needs before my own."

"There's nothing wrong with that. That's what family is for, don't you think?"

"I do. But not necessarily at the expense of twenty-five years. I feel like I wasted a lot of time trying to be everything to everyone. Sometimes a girl needs to take a chance and give herself time to be selfish."

"Is that why you said yes to me walking you home? It was time to be selfish?"

She thought about that, then shook her head. "Yes. Hmm. No, I mean, *nee*."

"Yes and no?"

"What I'm trying to say—very badly, I might add—is that I think I realized that there was something different about you. It appealed to me. I wanted to get to know you better."

"I think I was ready to be selfish, too, if you want to know the truth," Jacob said. "When I heard that my brother and sister-in-law died, it made me realize that I'd been living each day without much thought to the future, or to my past. I'd been living in Pinecraft, getting up in the morning, working my job, getting something quick to eat, and sleeping. And then doing it all over again in the morning."

She knew exactly what he was getting at. It was so easy to think that each day was going to be like the one before and the next one, too. Before you knew it, another week had passed, then a month. And if you weren't careful, you would have nothing to show for it.

"I'm not sure what I want to do with my life anymore," Rebecca admitted as they turned down her long driveway and headed toward the large white two-story house that her family had lived in for generations. "I thought it was caring for my siblings. Then I thought it was teaching school. But maybe God simply wants me to try to make a difference in other people's lives."

"That's all?" he asked in a teasing tone. "Attempting to make a difference is a pretty lofty goal to take on."

"Maybe. Or maybe not. You see, my mother was able to make a difference in our lives almost every day before she passed away." To her surprise, her throat got tight with emotion. Even after all this time, she still missed her mother's love and guidance.

"What did she do that was so special?"

"She raised a family. She cooked us supper every evening and made us breakfast every morning."

"Don't all mothers do that?"

She shrugged. "Maybe. But if you had asked me when I was seven if other mothers did that, I would have told you it didn't matter to me. All I cared about was that my mother did. She made a difference in my life."

"When you figure out what you are going to do, let me know. Because I am simply just trying to get through each day."

Rebecca nodded, but inside she felt deflated. Maybe she had been sounding just a little too preachy. Or perhaps she'd sounded dreamy? After all, it was a fairly big proposal, to attempt to make such a difference in a life.

She was just about to explain herself again when Jacob started laughing.

"When did you get that little guy?"

She slowly turned her head to where Jacob was staring and gasped.

There, in one of their flower beds stood a baby goat. It was a tiny thing, surely not more than a few months old. It seemed fascinated with Amelia's mums and was nibbling on the purple ones that lined the bed. By the looks of things, it had been enjoying those mums for quite a while.

As they got closer, it popped its head up, a ragged bloom hanging from its teeth, and stared directly at them. Rebecca couldn't help but smile. It was adorable with silky white fur, an inquisitive expression, and sturdy-looking little legs.

"You didn't tell me you'd gotten a baby goat," Jacob said. "It's cute."

"I didn't know, either." It was impossible to keep the dismay out of her voice. "I don't know where it came from."

"Well, it currently seems to have a fondness for purple chrysanthemums. I wonder why."

Intent on saving the mums her mother had planted years ago, Rebecca strode toward it. But she was brought up short by its change in expression. Instead of looking content, it now looked extremely irritated with her. Its beady black eyes looked directly at her.

Did goats bite? She wasn't sure. After a few seconds, it bleated.

Jacob, unfortunately, looked just as lost about what to do with the little creature as she did. He was standing in front of it, his hands held out, as if warding off an attack.

The goat? Well, after barely glancing at Jacob, it delicately pulled the head of yet another mum and began nibbling on it in earnest.

"Do you want me to try to grab hold of it?" Jacob asked.

"I don't know." If they caught the little thing, what would they do with it then? Maybe that didn't matter, though. She couldn't simply remain there and watch it destroy Amelia's garden.

"Oh, Princess. *Nee!*" Amelia cried as she ran out from the barn. "You mustn't eat the blooms." When she saw Rebecca, Amelia frowned at her. "Becky, why are you just watching Princess eat my garden?"

The answer seemed so obvious, she didn't dare say it. Instead, she asked a question of her own. "Why is a goat here? And why on earth is it named Princess?"

"She is my new kid," Amelia explained as she strode into the bed and wrapped her arms around the goat's neck. After brushing a hand through its soft-looking fur, she added, "I thought Princess was a wonderful-*gut* name. She's a rather fine-looking goat, don'tcha think?"

"She is pretty, I'll give you that," Rebecca said. "But I don't understand how she came to be here."

"Oh, that's easy. I was over at Hershberger's today and they had some goats for sale."

Hershberger's was a popular tourist destination in the area. Folks could even buy corn to feed the goats who loved standing on top of one of the barns. The place was fun and the goats were amusing to watch. But it was a bit of a shock to realize that Amelia had not only ventured over there on her own, but had chosen a baby goat, too.

Not wanting to hurt her sister's feelings, Rebecca took care to simply state the obvious. "So you bought one."

"Obviously," Amelia said as she pulled the goat toward Rebecca and Jacob. "Hi," she said with a smile. "We haven't met. I'm Amelia Kinsinger."

"Jacob Yoder."

Still holding on to the goat, she looked from Rebecca to Jacob and back. "Are you new to Charm?"

"*Jah*. Just moved here from Florida."

"His niece is in Rachel's classroom. That's how we met."

"I didn't think you were helping out there anymore."

"I'm not. But now Jacob is going to work at Kinsinger's."

"Are you? That's *gut* to know. Doing what?"

"Carpentry. I'll be building house frames," Jacob added.

Before Amelia could ask any more personal questions, Rebecca redirected their conversation back to the goat. "Where is, ah, Princess going to be living?"

"In the barn, of course." Looking a little worried, Amelia added, "But I think I'm going to need to get her in a better stall. She slipped out of the one I put her in just an hour ago."

"Let me see if I can help you," Jacob said.

Amelia smiled softly. "*Danke*. Lukas is going to be mighty upset with me if I don't make sure to take care of Princess."

"Does Lukas know about her yet?" Rebecca asked.

"Of course not."

"Aren't you a little worried he's gonna be upset?"

"*Nee.*" Looking decidedly obstinate, she added, "Lukas is my big brother, not my guardian."

That was true. However . . . "But don't you think you should have asked him about her?"

"*Nee.* Why? Are you upset that I didn't ask you?"

She was, actually. A flower-eating goat sounded like trouble. "I'm not upset," she began, "but I am surprised."

"You'll get used to Princess in no time," she said as she picked up the goat and started toward the barn. "*Danke* for your help, Jacob."

After sending an amused smile her way, Jacob turned to Rebecca. "I guess I should go help out your sister."

It was startling, but she felt a fresh burst of jealousy. Amelia, with her perfect balance of beauty and sweetness could get just about anyone to do anything for her. Especially if that someone was a man. Since it had been happening all their lives, probably from the time that Amelia could smile and point to a block or toy that she wanted, Rebecca couldn't even fault her sister for it.

But suddenly, Rebecca wished Amelia's natural appeal wasn't quite so . . . well, appealing. "You don't have to go help her if you don't want to," she said. "Lukas can work on the stall later."

"I don't mind helping." She bet he didn't. Just as she was willing herself not to say anything unkind, he added, "But would you do me a favor, too?"

"What do you need?"

"Come rescue me in fifteen minutes or so?"

Since he looked like the last man to ever need to be rescued, especially not from Amelia, she laughed. "What do you need rescuing from?"

"Princess. She's cute, but I'm not really a fan of goats."

"You really aren't a farmer, are you?"

Looking sheepish, he grinned. "Nope. Besides, no offense, but I didn't come here to work in your barn. I wanted to see you."

Instantly, all her worries vanished. "I'll come to the rescue in fifteen minutes."

"*Danke,*" he said before striding to the barn.

After watching him for a bit too long, Rebecca went inside the house. She needed to put her purse down and clean up.

Later, after she "rescued" Jacob, she was going to need to be ready to referee the inevitable argument that was going to take place between her siblings. Because no matter what Amelia thought, a new baby goat named Princess was absolutely the last thing their family needed.

# Chapter 18

This was not how Jacob had anticipated their evening would go.

He was currently kneeling in a patch of straw in a rather dark and dingy horse stall in the back of the Kinsingers' barn. While he hammered at a stretch of chicken wire across the bottom of the railing—which he seriously doubted would keep a rambunctious goat out of trouble—the tiny goat had taken to amusing herself by nibbling on his pant leg.

Furthermore, the person he was there for, the one person in all of Charm whom he was eager to know a whole lot better, was nowhere to be found.

Instead, her sister, Amelia, was in the stall with him. She was sitting on an old barrel as casually as if she'd been sitting with a group of women sipping tea. And between looking over his shoulder and giving him instructions he didn't need, she was doing a very bad job of controlling one playful, hungry goat.

Princess seemed to have forgotten all about her penchant for chrysanthemums and now was fixated on chewing a hole in the hem of his trousers. She was as determined to get her way as a toddler on a quest for a forbidden toy.

Every time Amelia pulled her away with something silly like, "Oh, *nee*, Princess," the goat bleated a bit, glared at Amelia, and scooted closer to him again.

Jacob was fairly certain that he was going to go home with a big hole in his pants. Disciplining the goat itself was not an option. Instead, he did his best to concentrate on creating a safe spot for Princess as quickly as possible. Then he could get out of this stall and get back to the reason he was there in the first place.

"Jacob, how do you think it looks?" Amelia asked. "Do you think it's gonna be Princess-proof?"

"I hope so." And he really meant that. But based on Princess's behavior so far he doubted it would stand up against her for longer than ten minutes.

"I hope so, too. She's going to need to learn to like her little stall, because I don't think either Rebecca or Lukas is going to let her inside the house."

She sounded almost serious. Turning around, he looked at her. "You actually want this goat to live in your *haus*?"

Her lips twitched. "Not really. But it's fun to think about. Ain't so?"

Princess head-butted him. He fell from his crouch and landed on the exact spot that Princess had apparently had in mind. "I think it would only be fun for a certain goat," he teased.

As the silly animal scooted closer and craned her neck for a rub and he complied, Amelia giggled. "She's won you over, too. I knew she would."

Smiling at her, he had to admit that it wasn't just the goat who had done that, it was Amelia, too. Now that the goat wasn't tearing at his clothes, he could get a better look at Rebecca's sister. Even in the dim light, Jacob was certain that Amelia was the prettiest woman he'd ever seen. Blessed with light blond hair, pure blue eyes, a heart-shaped face, and a lithe figure, all matched by a sweet personality, she was truly lovely.

Part of him was surprised he wasn't thinking about her. She was sweet, pretty, and unattached. But he wasn't interested in developing anything more with her than a friendship. Instead, his heart and thoughts were thoroughly concentrating on one person and that was Amelia's sister.

"I am fairly sure this goat did not win me over, Amelia."

"She might have." After placing a kiss on the goat's head she added, "I knew she was the goat for me as soon as I saw her in the pen at Hershberger's."

"You knew she was the goat for you?" he repeated with a smile.

"She trotted right up to me and stayed by my side. She liked me from the moment we saw each other."

Jacob didn't know much about goats, but he was fairly certain little goats didn't bond with young women that quickly. Not even pretty blondes like Amelia. "You are too silly," he teased, feeling like his life would have been even better if he'd had a little sister like Amelia around when he was growing up.

"I'm not silly, Jake. I only know what I like."

"And you like goats."

"It's true."

When she let out a giggle, he laughed, too. He could only imagine what a handful Amelia had been for her siblings.

He was just about to finish up the project when the barn door opened and Lukas Kinsinger walked in. He was followed by a man of similar build but with light brown eyes and darker brown hair. They were deep in conversation, then turned in unison to the stall that he, Amelia, and one goat occupied.

Both men stopped and stared.

Amelia raised a hand. "Hiya, Lukas."

Her brother looked thoroughly confused. The other man appeared just plain irritated.

Striding over, Lukas said, "Hi there, Jacob. When I hired you for the lumberyard, I never thought I could hire you to work in my barn, too. Is there a special reason I'm finding you hammering chicken wire in here?"

There was no way he was going to try to explain himself while crouched on the other side of a horse stall. He stood up. "I was simply doing a favor for Amelia."

The other man approached and rested his elbows on the top rung on the stall. "Oh? And what kind of favor was that?"

Jacob knew that tone, and he wasn't about to get involved in a fight over Amelia. He raised his hands. "Obviously, I'm hammering chicken wire. Nothing more."

"Settle, Simon," Lukas murmured. "Jacob, this here is Simon Hochstetler. He's a *gut* friend and one of my supervisors at the mill. Simon, this is Jacob Yoder. He was just hired on over in Marcus's section."

"Hi, Simon. It's *gut* to meet you," Jacob said.

The other man simply glared, then said, "That doesn't tell me why you are alone in the Kinsingers' barn with Amelia."

Jacob was too old to be cowed by another man's jealousy. And it was mighty obvious that's what this was. "I already told you what I was doing. Nothing more. Nothing less." Unless one counted his pant leg getting chewed by a billy goat.

"Because?"

Wearing a determined expression, Amelia strode forward. "Because I got a goat today. That's why."

"That goat is ours?"

"Absolutely."

Lukas groaned. "Amelia, why ever would you do that?"

"Because I wanted one." Looking at Princess fondly, she said, "Isn't she sweet?"

"That ain't how I would describe her, Amy." Sounding more irritated by the minute, he asked, "What are you going to do with her? Make goat's-milk cheese?"

Her smile faltered. "Of course not." Looking warily at both Simon and Jacob, she said, "I think it would be a *gut* idea if we talked about this later. When we are alone."

"*Nee*, let's get this over with now."

"But Lukas—"

"I'm not asking you to reveal any dark secrets, sister," he said impatiently. "I simply want to know why—with everything else going on—that you decided to buy this . . . this . . ."

"It's a goat," she inserted. "It's a tiny baby goat and it needed a home. She's going to be my pet." Raising her chin, she added, "And I suggest you remember who you are talking to, *bruder*. I'm your sister, not your employee."

Lukas pulled his hat off his head and ran his fingers through his very short reddish-blond hair. Around a groan he said, "Amelia, really?"

Just like that, her expression crumbled.

It was so disheartening to watch that Jacob was tempted to intervene, even though he didn't really know Amelia at all and Lukas was his new boss. It was obvious, to him at least, that the woman had had enough and was about to dissolve into tears.

But before he could say a word, Simon spoke. "That's enough, Luke."

Lukas turned to stare at his friend. "What?"

Stepping closer, Simon said, "You heard me. You are being a bull-headed jerk. Don't browbeat your sister for having a kind heart. There's nothing wrong with that."

Lukas raised his brows. "When did you become the expert on tender hearts?"

"I don't need to be an expert to know that you are overstepping. She is exactly right. You're her brother, not her father. Plus, Amelia is here all day by herself."

"I canna help that. I've got a mill to run."

"What I am trying to say is that while Levi is off discovering himself or something, most of the burden of the house and farm is on Amelia. I think if she wants a tiny white goat to fuss over, then she should have it."

"I didn't ask for your opinion."

"But you should have." After giving Lukas a steady glare, he added, "Lukas, you are a good man and a *gut bruder*. I know you care. But that don't mean you are always right."

"Lukas, it will be all right," Amelia said in a rush. "I promise, you won't hardly know Princess is here."

"Princess?"

Lukas looked so incredulous, Jacob was tempted to laugh. With effort he remained quiet and tried to blend in with the woodwork while the drama spun out around him.

Ignoring Lukas's outburst, Simon held out a hand. "Come on, Amy. Let's get you out of the horse's stall. It looks like Jacob has almost gotten all the chicken wire up."

"I should stay here and help," she said.

"He doesn't need your help," Simon retorted. "If he needs a

hand, Lukas here can help." With another glare, he said, "That's what brothers do, *jah*?"

Amelia patted the goat before sliding through the stall door, and Simon looked at Luke. "I'm going to take her for a walk. We'll be back in an hour or so."

As Lukas narrowed his eyes, Rebecca entered the barn. And boy, did she look angry. "Simon, I thought we already talked about this."

Still guiding Amelia out of the stall, he shrugged. "Just because you talked doesn't mean that I had to listen, Becky."

Looking at everyone assembled around them, Amelia seemed even more ill at ease. "Simon, *danke*, but I'm starting to think that maybe I should stay here. I don't want Princess to be any trouble."

"It's a goat, not a baby, Amy," Simon said in a firm tone. "She won't be any trouble. And you need a little break from this place. You've been here all day." Turning to Lukas, Simon said, "Don't you agree?"

Lukas rolled his eyes. "*Jah*. Sure." Softening his tone, he said, "Simon is right, Amy. I overreacted. Get on out of here for a bit. Princess will be fine."

Looking thoroughly relieved, Amelia gazed up at Simon. "*Danke.*"

Simon stared at Amelia with a tender expression. "Never thank me for wanting to spend time with you. We're friends, right?"

"Oh. Of course."

As Jacob looked at Lukas and Rebecca, he couldn't help but think that they had a reason to be perturbed. Amelia might think she and Simon were just friends, but there was nothing in Simon's manner or speech that made anyone think he felt the same way. On the contrary, it was starting to be fairly obvious that mere friendship was probably the very last thing Simon had in mind for Amelia Kinsinger.

When Amelia and Simon were gone, Lukas glared at Jacob, then at the goat, then kind of threw up his hands. "I'm going inside to see Darla," he said as he strode out of the barn.

Jacob rested his arms on the top of the stall. "You look a little irritated, Rebecca. You all right?"

"Honestly? I don't know." She opened her mouth to say something, then seemed to change her mind. "Are you okay?"

Before he could answer, Princess butted him on his calf. When he looked down and saw the little white goat gazing up at him with something that looked a lot like happiness, he crouched down and rubbed her neck and chest. "I'm *gut*. Come here and see this little thing."

He thought she might refuse, but when she got right in the stall with him, knelt down, and tentatively petted the goat only to be rewarded with a gentle head butt, she smiled. "She's mighty sweet. I don't know if I'd call her Princess, but I'm starting to understand why Amelia fell in love with her."

"Sometimes good things just kind of sneak up on you. Ain't so?"

"*Jah*," she said after a moment's consideration. "You are exactly right."

Later, after Jacob finished securing Princess's new home, said good-bye to Rebecca, and began his long walk home, he realized that he was glad the afternoon had been so full of events. It had been good and it had surely snuck up on him.

He couldn't wait to walk Rebecca home again.

# Chapter 19

*Wednesday, September 16*

It had now been three weeks since Marcus had asked Rachel to quit and she'd ignored him. And it was now one week since Rebecca had informed her that she would no longer be helping out in the classroom.

As she walked home at the end of another school day, Rachel knew that both her time and her options were running out. Marcus had become increasingly frustrated with her. He claimed he wanted her to quit because of her health, but she wasn't positive that was the reason. Something more was bothering him. Unfortunately, she wasn't sure what it could be. She'd tried several times to draw him out, to ask him about both the accident at the mill and his worries about Agnes. However, each time, he cut her off.

She needed to confide in someone before she blurted something unkind to Marcus or made herself sick with worry.

Deciding that there was no time like the present, she turned down one of the small side streets off of Main and headed home.

Not to the home she shared with Marcus. Instead, to the one she'd grown up in. The house that had always been filled with laughter and was never quite tidy. Her mother—much to her father's amusement—was the type to start multiple projects and work on them at the same time. Because of that, there were always half-finished quilts, sewing projects, a cookbook she'd been attempting to write for three years, and a half dozen other items scattered in each room.

As Rachel walked up the front walkway and saw a pile of un-folded laundry lying forgotten on a chair by the door, a basket of clothespins keeping it company, she laughed. Some things never changed.

She opened the screen door without knocking and fol-lowed the sound of chatter through the house until she found her mother and her sister Carrie in Carrie's old room. Carrie's daughter Bliss was in her sister's arms, playing with a teeth-ing ring. Surrounding them were plastic grocery bags of quilt scraps.

Rachel grinned to herself. If Marcus saw the mess, he'd say that it looked like a quilt had exploded. It really was a mess.

"Rachel, look at you!" her mother said as she got up and en-folded her in a warm hug. "How are you feeling?"

"Better," she replied. She knew Carrie and Mamm would think she was referring to her recent morning sickness, but she was actually talking about her mood. She loved being home, and her mother's hugs were always the best.

Her mother had never been especially slim or even especially pretty. She'd once told Rachel that she used to be sad that she was such a "Plain Jane" when she'd been a teenager. She said she'd always wished that her eyes were a prettier shade of brown or that her eyebrows were arched better or that she had more prominent cheekbones.

But none of that had ever seemed to bother Daed. He always said that he'd fancied Margaret Miller from the first moment he'd spied her.

After greeting Carrie and Bliss, she sat down on the bed next to them. "What are you doing?"

"We're going to have a quilt auction at the beginning of December to help some widows over in Walnut Creek. I was telling Carrie that the auction was a perfect excuse to use up some of these scraps."

Rachel had never been a skilled quilter, but she knew enough to be skeptical about fabric scraps. There were a lot of scraps, but not enough of each to make any kind of uniform design. At least, she didn't think so. "What pattern are ya going to do?"

Carrie grinned. "We're thinking crazy quilts. Want to help?"

"Maybe. I don't know."

Her mother patted her arm. "Don't worry, child. I know you don't have time for this. You've got Marcus, a *boppli* to prepare for, and a class of *kinner* to teach."

That easy reminder seemed to be all she needed to lose her composure. Tears filled her eyes before she could stop them.

"Uh-oh. What did I say?"

"Marcus wants me to quit," she blurted. "But I don't want to."

Carrie leaned back, picked up a box of tissues from one of the bedside tables, and handed it to her. "Of course you'll have to quit when you have your babe, Rachel. Everyone does."

"I know. Even though I wish that wasn't true, I know."

Her mother and sister exchanged glances. "Then why are you crying?" Carrie asked.

"Marcus wants me to quit *now*." Around a hiccup, she added, "Actually, he wanted me to quit a couple of weeks ago."

"Why does he want that?" Mamm asked. "He must know that the children and their parents are counting on you."

And there the tears came again. "He doesn't care. He's been so different since I told him I was pregnant. He acted surprised that it happened so quickly, and now wants me to stay home all day long and get a 'real' doctor instead of Agnes."

"Oh, boy," Mamm said.

Grabbing another tissue from the box her sister had just handed her, Rachel nodded. "I don't know what to do. I don't want to disobey Marcus but I don't want to do everything he wants me to do either."

"What have you been doing?" Carrie asked. "Did you teach today?"

"*Jah*. I told him that I needed a few more weeks. But he's losing patience."

Her mother's pretty brown eyes warmed with compassion. "You are so upset! You should have come over to talk to me weeks ago."

"I didn't think talking about Marcus was the right thing to do."

Carrie rolled her eyes. "Your husband is a handsome man and a good one, too. But that don't mean he's perfect, Rachel. Take it from me, sometimes husbands need to be managed a bit. Once you do that, they will start to do what you want them to."

"You manage Tim?"

"Of course. And if Bethany were here, she'd tell you the same thing about Graham. So would Joy. Her Stephen would be lost without her."

"And Paul?" She didn't think her brother would enjoy being managed.

Her mother laughed. "If our Paul ever gets married, I think he will welcome being managed. Of all my *kinner*, God gave him my penchant for unfinished projects." Still looking amused, her mother hopped off the bed. "Let's go get you a snack. You've got to be hungry."

"I kinda am," she said sheepishly. "I was so worried at lunch, I didn't eat much."

As they walked to the kitchen, Carrie said, "I think you should pick your battles, sister. Tell Marcus that you will gladly go to the doctor instead of Agnes."

"But Agnes delivered Bliss."

"*Jah*, but it wasn't an easy delivery. Tim asked me to have our future children in the hospital." Looking at her sympathetically, she said, "It wasn't a hard thing to agree to, Rachel. Tim just wanted me and the babe to be safe."

"I guess that makes sense," she said as they entered the kitchen.

"It does," Mamm said as she bustled around the large, cluttered kitchen. "Marcus loves you. Now, go sit down."

Rachel sat on one of the red barstools that surrounded the butcher-block island. "I think Marcus is still dealing with the accident at the mill," she said quietly. "He won't talk about that day or the fire, but sometimes I see him staring off into space looking sad."

"It makes sense that he's still struggling. It was a terrible day," her mother said as she set a plate of sliced apples, some gingersnaps, and a glass of milk in front of Rachel.

It was the same snack she'd made for all of them when they got home from school. "Mamm, I'm a teacher now, you know. This is the snack you gave me when we were little."

"It's still a good one. Now drink your milk."

Obediently, she did as she was told. By the time she finished her milk and had cleaned most of her plate, Rachel realized that she felt much better. "*Danke*. I should be getting on home now. Marcus will worry."

"Want me to leave Bliss with Mamm and walk you home?" Carrie asked. "We can talk some more about things."

"*Nee*. I think I'm going to be all right. I'm going to tell Marcus that I'll start going to the real doctor, but that I want to teach until the doctor says I shouldn't."

Carrie grinned. "That sounds like a good plan."

"I'll pray for you, too, dear," her mother said. "And I'm going to start coming up to school once a week to help you clean up your room and walk home with ya, too."

"That's not necessary."

"It is for me," she said as she treated Rachel to another warm hug. "You are my youngest. And even though you're all grown-up and married, something tells me that I'm going to always worry about you."

As she walked out the door and headed to her new home, Rachel realized that she was grateful for her mother's concern and her sister's advice. It felt good to know that she had them, no matter what happened.

# Chapter 20

*Friday, September 18*

S o, what did you think of last night's homework?" Meghan, Lilly's high school tutor, asked.

    Soon after her family had decided to allow Lilly to be tutored, her teacher had invited Meghan to stop by the Amish school to meet Lilly. They'd immediately hit it off. Meghan came over the next day to tutor her. So far, they'd had four sessions. Meghan was earning school credit for tutoring Lilly so she was available to come to the school every couple of days.

They'd decided during their first tutoring session to work outside, apart from the other kids, and now they had a pretty good routine. If they attempted to work together in a corner of the room, too many people focused on what they were doing instead of their own assignments.

For her part, Lilly loved the opportunity to work outside in the open. She also loved having Meghan's attention completely on her. Meghan's perceptiveness and many questions challenged Lilly in a way that she never had been before.

Now, as they settled into their usual spots at the picnic table, Lilly thought about homework that Meghan had assigned. "It was hard."

"Too hard?"

"*Nee*," Lilly answered with a sheepish smile. "Just hard enough."

"I'm glad about that." As Meghan opened up her backpack and started taking out supplies, she filled Lilly in on everything that she'd been doing since they'd met last.

Her chattiness was one of the reasons Lilly enjoyed working with her so much. Meghan was a senior. Her stories about applying for college and the antics at her part-time job at the Homestead Restaurant were always entertaining. She also always had a story about her boyfriend, the past weekend's football game, or her little sisters.

And she was really smart. She could answer Lilly's questions without having to look up answers and explained things well. Their time together always passed too quickly.

"Before we get started, what did you think about the science book I left for you?"

"That was harder, but I did okay." Biting her bottom lip, she said, "I mean, at least I think I did okay. I memorized a good bit of the periodic tables, though I'm not really sure what knowing the symbol for magnesium is going to do for me."

Meghan pressed a hand to her chest in her usual dramatic way. "Lilly, you're wounding me! You're supposed to think that everything I am teaching you is worthwhile."

"I'm trying for it to be." She grinned then.

"Trying? Try harder."

Lilly laughed.

"Lucky for you, Lilly Yoder, that I came prepared for my know-it-all student." Meghan reached into her book bag and pulled out one very big textbook.

Lilly looked at it with some misgiving. It looked heavy and hard. Not a good combination. "Uh-oh. What is that?"

"Chemistry." Meghan grinned like she'd just announced the best thing, ever. "Yesterday, I talked to my physics teacher about you and she gave me suggestions of what we should tackle next." Looking at Lilly with a gleam in her eye, she added, "What do you think? Are you ready to tackle freshman chem?"

Flipping through the pages, Lilly bit her bottom lip again. "I'm not sure. This all looks pretty complicated."

"That's why you have me, silly girl. We're going to do this together. I would never make you work on it alone."

Lilly smiled and couldn't help but think that what Meghan said was true. Now that she'd opened herself up to accepting and asking for help, everything was becoming easier.

"Lead the way, then, Meghan. I'm all ears."

"You are too cute." The high school girl grinned as she flipped to a new page on their spiral notebook and opened up the text-book to the first lesson. "Now," she began, "the first thing you need to know is the difference between organic and inorganic chemistry."

Lilly wrote that down. Then thought about nothing but what Meghan was teaching for the next hour and a half. In many ways, it was the fastest ninety minutes of her life.

"So, how did it go today?" Peter asked after school when they were walking back home. "Did you learn anything new?"

Lilly grinned. He always asked that. Ever since he realized that she'd already learned what Mrs. Mast was teaching and wanted to learn new things, too, he acted like her education was the most important thing in the world.

She thought it was very sweet.

"Meghan decided that we needed to start chemistry today. So that's what we did." Holding out her book bag, she said, "Feel this."

He grabbed ahold of it, then looked at it in shock when he realized how heavy it was. "What did she give you? Rocks?"

After setting the bag on the dirt path, she dug out her new textbook. "It's a giant chemistry book. From the high school."

"What are you going to do with that besides get sore arms?"

"Ha-ha," she said as she bent down to place it back in her tote. "I guess I'm gonna learn chemistry."

"Why? What will you do with that?"

"Actually, I have no idea. I guess one day I'll figure that out."

He smiled. "I bet you will."

She'd just picked up her bag when he held out his arm. "Give me that."

"Peter, I can carry my own bag."

"I can, too."

"But there's no need."

"Lilly, I'm here, I'm stronger. Let me, okay?"

Since it was probably past time to give in gracefully, she nodded. "Thank you." As they started walking back on the path between the two farms, Lilly looked at Peter. "What about you?" she asked.

"What about me?"

"Come on. I'm tired of us always talking about me. What did you do in class today?"

He shrugged, and his expression shuttered. "Nothing too special. Just the regular stuff."

"Don't you want to talk about it?" She never wanted him to think that she wasn't interested in him, too.

"Not really. I got most of my work done, which was all I really care about." Puffing up his chest, he said, "I'm working at Kinsinger's today."

"Again?" She was surprised. "You worked yesterday. I thought you only worked a day or two each week."

"*Nee*, I *used* to only work a day or two each week. Now I am working four." Looking really proud of himself, he said, "Mr. Kinsinger himself talked to me on Monday about taking a new position at the mill."

"What are you going to be doing?"

Peter stopped. Turning to her, he smiled. It was a beautiful smile, one that made her realize that while he often looked amused, he didn't often look truly happy.

"I'm gonna be a runner," he said.

"What does a runner do?"

"You see, most of the employees are taught to work on computers when they are hired. But Mr. K. said some of the men aren't liking that method real well. They miss interacting with people or something. Because of that, I'm going to deliver different messages and such around the offices and warehouses a couple of times an afternoon."

"It sounds kind of fun."

He nodded. "*Jah*. I think so, too. Plus, I'm going to meet a lot of important people there. Most of my messages are going to go to the team leaders and those are the men who do a lot of the hiring. If a couple of the men there take a liking to me, I won't have to worry about getting full-time work as soon as school gets out."

She felt a little dismayed, though she carefully tamped down that emotion. "You don't like school, do you?"

"It's not that I don't like it, I am just tired of it."

"It's a blessing that you've found someplace where you want to work."

"*Jah*. It is." Looking really pleased, he added, "I can't wait to work there full-time."

"Guess what? My uncle Jacob is working at the lumber mill now, too. He really hated farming."

"I heard he was there. Someone said that some of the old men farmers in the area were making fun of him. Is that why he stopped?"

"*Nee*. Oncle Jake doesn't let other people's opinions bother him too much. He told me that he just knew that God hadn't given him a farmer's mentality. He didn't understand how to read the soil and crops and such. Plus, he hated working alone every day."

"I would hate that, too."

"My uncle said he was meant to be a carpenter."

"It sounds like it."

They were at Main Street now. To the right was the way to her grandparents' farm. To the left was Kinsinger's Lumber Mill.

Lilly was startled that their afternoon walk had happened in a flash. How come time with Peter always went by far too quickly? "I guess this is where we say good-bye." She held out a hand. "You better hand me my book bag."

"Here you go," he said as he handed it to her. "But do you have to say good-bye just yet?"

"Well, no . . ."

"Want to come to the mill with me? You could go inside and see what it looks like." Peter brightened. "Maybe you could say hi to your uncle."

"I don't want to bother him."

Eyes sparkling, Peter said, "You could see Miss Rebecca, too. She's at the reception desk." He lowered his voice. "Everyone says your uncle and her are sweet on each other."

"I know they're friends," she said hesitantly. Although, to be sure, she'd seen both Rebecca and her uncle stare at each other when they thought no one was looking.

"They're more than that," Peter said confidently. "I think they might be a real couple now."

Lilly gaped at him. But then, as Peter's words sank in, she realized he was probably right. Furthermore, she kind of thought it made sense. Both her uncle and Rebecca had experienced loss yet still carried a positive attitude with them wherever they went. "If that's the truth, I think it might be a good idea to say hello," she said with a smile.

"*Gut.* Now we don't have to say good-bye to each other yet."

Lilly didn't add anything, but she was secretly glad about that, too.


"Rebecca," Lukas called out, "did we ever hear from the shipment that's late out of northern Michigan?"

"We did. It should be here within the hour."

"And did you talk to Roman about the famous football player who wanted him to design two enormous front doors?"

"Not yet," she answered as the front door opened and Peter and Lilly walked in. "But Peter just got here. I'll ask him to do it."

Lukas, who had been standing in his doorway as was his habit, both talking to her and anyone else who walked by at the same time, grinned. "Peter, you are exactly who I need to see."

Peter raised his brows. "Any reason why?"

"*Jah*," Lukas said, "I've got a list of things for you to do about a mile long."

Peter's lips curved up. "Don't know if I'll get everything done, but I'll do my best."

Lukas grinned. "*Gut*, because I've got to tell ya that every team leader has taken time to tell me that he's impressed with you. Watch out, son. You're well on your way to becoming indispensable."

"I'm not real sure what that means," Peter quipped, "but I'm hoping it means something good."

"It means they are starting to depend on you, Peter," Lilly said.

Rebecca watched the boy pull back his shoulders and nod importantly.

"I'll do whatever you need me to do."

As Lukas's gaze drifted toward Lilly, he raised a brow. "Any special reason you decided to bring your girlfriend to work?"

Lilly's eyes widened. She also flushed from her hairline to her toes.

"*Nee*," Peter sputtered. "This here is Lilly Yoder. Her uncle just started working here. She wanted to say hi to Rebecca."

Lukas looked even more confused. "Why Rebecca?"

"I think I'd better leave," Lilly whispered.

"*Nee*, stay!" Rebecca called out. Getting to her feet and circling around the desk, she said, "Lilly, I'm so sorry. My *bruder* doesn't always say things in the best way. He's teasing you, I promise."

Lilly relaxed. "Oh."

Peter had taken a step closer to the girl. Rebecca thought his protectiveness was quite sweet. She just wished her brother would sometimes stop being so bossy.

Turning to Lukas, Rebecca said, "I met Lilly when I was volunteering. And you know Jacob. He's our new hire for shells. You know, from Pinecraft. Now, be nice."

"Oh. Now I understand." Looking far less scary, Lukas smiled Lilly's way. "It's *gut* to meet you, Lilly. Do you want me to send your uncle out front?"

"*Nee.*" After darting a look at Peter, she said, "I don't know why I came here with him."

"I'm glad you did," Rebecca said. "Do you have time to have a snack or a drink? The café is open upstairs."

"I have time."

"*Gut.* All right, then. Let me go see if Mercy can come take my place. Then you and I can get a cool drink and visit for a few moments before I go back to work," she added, just in case Lukas was going to start worrying that she was done for the day.

Lukas rocked back on his heels. "Now that Lilly is settled, Peter, come with me. I'm gonna write out a note I want you to give to Roman in woodworking. Then, I've got another job for ya, too." As was his way, he was talking and walking at the same time. "Hey, do you have a locker yet?"

"I do," Peter said as he looked back at Lilly.

"*Gut.* Go put up your things while I write out the note," Lukas called out from his office.

"See ya, Lilly," Peter said.

"Bye," she said, blushing again. But this time, Rebecca noticed that her blush wasn't from embarrassment, it was from something far different.

Fifteen minutes later, Rebecca had the chance to ask Lilly about that blush. Mercy had stepped into Rebecca's place for the next hour. Therefore, Rebecca was going to have time to visit with Lilly as long as the girl wanted to.

After ordering a small sandwich and some lemonade, Lilly looked around the café with interest. "I thought there would be more workers here. Onkle Jake says Kinsinger's is a big place."

"It is. It's so big that we have three break rooms for the employees. The biggest is in the retail building, two others are near the collection of warehouses in the back. This café usually just serves customers or vendors. But I like to come up here, too, from time to time. It's nice that we have a place to order something good to eat."

"The sandwich is good."

"I'm glad." Rebecca smiled. "So, how is school going? Mrs. Mast told me that you are a mighty smart girl."

Lilly grinned. "Mrs. Mast connected me with some tutors from the high school. I'm learning chemistry now!"

Rebecca had no idea what chemistry entailed but she was glad that Lilly's eyes were shining when she talked about it. "And it seems that everything with you and Peter is going well?"

"*Jah*. We are good friends."

"Just *gut* friends?" Rebecca was fairly sure that Peter thought of Lilly a bit differently.

"Well, we're close. But we're not boyfriend and girlfriend." Looking worried, she added, "My grandparents wouldn't like that. I don't think Uncle Jacob would, either. Please don't tell him about us."

"I won't say anything. But I have to share that if you are happy with your new friend, I'm happy. It's hard moving to a new place. It's even harder finding happiness when one has suffered so much loss."

Lilly nodded.

Rebecca was tempted to reach out and clasp Lilly's hand but she was afraid the girl might find it off-putting. Instead, she said, "I am glad you are settling in."

"My uncle is, too," Lilly volunteered. "He seems a lot happier now that he's working at Kinsinger's."

"That's *gut* to know, too." Thinking about how their paths crossed, she added, "Funny how the Lord was working with both him and me at the same time! Both of us were trying to fit in where we didn't belong, Jacob with farming and me with teaching."

"He's said much the same thing to me."

Rebecca smiled. "Like you and Peter, he has become a good friend."

"I heard he's walked you home a couple of times."

Now Rebecca was certain that she was the one blushing. "He has. I'm far too old for that, I think."

"I don't think so." She shrugged. "Besides, it doesn't matter if you're too old or not, as long as something makes you happy."

"Those are wise words."

Lilly grinned. "I am a pretty smart girl."

"So modest, too," Rebecca teased. She was enjoying their time together so much.

She also had a pretty good idea that Lilly would adore Amelia.

Amelia had that perfect combination of motherliness and irreverence that Lilly would likely find irresistible. After all, Amelia also lost her mother at a young age.

Thinking of Oscar and Princess the goat, Rebecca decided she knew of just the right way to lure Lilly over to the house. "Lilly, did you know we have both a puppy and a baby goat at our house?"

"I heard Onkle Jacob fixed the goat's pen." Lilly's eyes were dancing.

"Would you like to come over sometime and see the animals? The goat is Amelia's, but the bulldog pup is mine. They are both mighty friendly."

"Do you mean you want me to come over with my uncle?"

"You can come with him, or by yourself, or . . . hey, I know, how about all of you come over on Saturday night? Your grandparents, too."

"I could ask them."

"Please do. It would be fun to have all of you over. *Wunderbaar.*"

Looking at her carefully, Lilly nodded. "I think so, too. I'll ask Mommi and Dawdi."

"Just send back word with either Peter or Jacob."

"I will do that," Lilly said with a smile.

Rebecca smiled back but felt as if Lilly was holding a secret. She wondered what it was.

# Chapter 21

*Saturday, September 19*

Rebecca Kinsinger's invitation might as well have come from the Bishop himself. It had thrown Jacob's parents into such a tizzy, his mother, especially.

Looking at the basket filled with fresh bread, canned pickles, and an apple-rhubarb pie, Jacob knew something had to be said. He didn't know a whole lot about social graces, but he was pretty sure that arriving to a dinner party with so much food was rude. "Mamm, they didn't ask us to bring anything. You can't show up at their doorstep with all of this."

"Why?"

"Because it's practically an entire meal. Rebecca's going to think you think that she can't cook."

"She's not going to think that."

"She might. Or her sister, Amelia, might. I got the impression Amelia wears her heart on her sleeve. You might offend her."

"I won't. Now, settle down, son. It ain't a meal. Just a couple of baked goods." Looking a bit put-upon, she added, "I have never heard of visiting a house without bringing a dish. It ain't done."

Now that he'd said his piece, Jacob knew better than to continue arguing his point. He was never going to win when the topic involved baked goods and hostess gifts. "We better get going. What can I help you carry to the buggy?"

"The whole basket, son," Daed called out with a grin. "And be quick about it. We decided it would be a *gut* idea to walk there."

Walk? "It's a good half hour walk for me." He didn't add the obvious—that it would be even longer for his parents. And that it was warm. And that they were already verging on being late. "Are you sure it wouldn't be better to take the buggy? It might turn dark by the time we head home."

But his father was not deterred. "Your mother and I have been walking in the dark for quite a while, Jacob. Plus, the good Lord gave us feet. We might as well use them."

Looking at the basket filled to the brim, Jacob was starting to think he was going to get to put his arms to work, too.

"All right. If you want to walk, we need to get started before we're too late. Let's go then."

"Lilly, come along now, child," his mother said.

"I'm ready!" Lilly called out from her room down the hall. "I'll be right there." Seconds later they heard her door slam.

Stunned, Jacob looked at his parents, who were wearing happy expressions. Well, his father was. His mother looked on the verge of tears.

"That's the first time since she moved in that she's acted like a child," she whispered. "Jacob, did ya hear that door slam?"

"I did." He decided not to point out that he and Marc used to get in trouble whenever they slammed doors.

"She sounds happy," his mother added, clasping her hands together. "Thank the good Lord."

"She sounds like her father used to," Daed added. "He loved to get together with friends."

A bolt of sadness struck Jacob hard. His father was right— Marc had been the one who loved making plans and getting together with other people. Jacob had always been the brother who had been perfectly happy to sit at home with a newspaper, book, or new project. Marc had loved being with other people and they'd loved being with him.

And now he was gone.

He pushed those dark thoughts away when he heard Lilly's footsteps. Picking up the basket, he pretended to groan at its weight. "Lilly, how are your muscles?"

"They are good." Eyeing the basket with a look of worry, she said, "Why?"

"Why? Well, I'm just trying to figure out if you're strong enough to . . ." He paused dramatically.

"Strong enough to what?"

"Help me carry this here basket of your *grandmommi's*? You're young and strong."

"I am young but not that strong." Plucking off the loaf of bread from the top of the basket, she shook her head. "I think my arms are only strong enough to carry bread and rolls."

"Daed, want to carry a pie?"

"I do not. Now, enough with your whining, son. Let's go, and step lively."

Jacob gestured for his parents and niece to go through first, then closed the door behind them. At last, they were on their way.

To his surprise, his parents strode ahead, practically race-walking toward the large Kinsinger property.

Lilly, however, stayed by his side. She was chatty, too. As they walked, stopping every ten minutes or so so he could switch the basket from one hand to the other, she told him about Meghan and her new textbook and Katie and something called inertia.

He nodded and tried to ask appropriate questions, but the truth was that she could talk about anything and he would think it was wonderful. She was just that happy.

When they climbed the crest of the last hill before they reached the Kinsingers', Lilly smiled at him yet again. "I'm really glad we're all together and going over there," she said.

"I am, too, sweetheart. I am, too."

"HONESTLY, THE WAY you are fussing over the table, you would think that we've never had company before," Lukas griped to Darla and Rebecca.

"We haven't had anyone over in a long time," Rebecca said.

"Certainly not since I've been living here," Darla added.

Lukas frowned. "Sure we have. Darla, we had Patsy and Gretel over two nights ago."

"They weren't company. They're my sisters," Darla said.

"They still count."

"Not as special company."

"Mr. and Mrs. Yoder are going to be here," Rebecca tried to explain. Again. "That is different."

"Why? They're only Jacob's parents."

When Darla rolled her eyes, Lukas folded his arms across his chest and glared at Rebecca. "What? I thought we were simply being neighborly. Is there a certain reason we are hosting them that I don't know about?"

If there was, she certainly wasn't going to confess it to her brother! "I invited them over because it's the nice thing to do."

He narrowed his eyes. "I don't think so."

"Oh, for heaven's sakes. You know why Rebecca invited everyone over, Luke," Darla said with a playful slap on his arm. "Don't fuss at her so much."

Pressing a hand to his wife's tiny waist, he smiled fondly at her. After she smiled back, obviously sharing some kind of special, silent communication, he turned back to Rebecca. "Care to tell me how serious the two of you are?"

"Uh, *nee*. I do not."

"I'm your older brother. I should know these things."

After darting a look at Darla, who shrugged, Rebecca decided to go ahead and be honest. "I don't actually know how serious we are."

"Why not?"

"Because neither of us have made any big declarations, *bruder*."

"He's been walking you home." Lukas raised his brows, just as if Rebecca had been doing something so scandalous that the whole town should be worried.

"*Jah*. He's been walking me home. But like I said, we haven't had any big heart-to-heart talks in the middle of the alfalfa fields."

"Tell me, then. Do you like him a lot? Are you falling in love? Do you think he's the man for you?"

"Lukas, oh my heavens. Stop." Looking at Darla for support, Rebecca exclaimed, "Do something!"

"He kind of has the right to ask," Darla said. "I mean, he is the head of your household."

Feeling like her cheeks were on fire, she turned to Amelia, who had just entered the dining room but had remained suspiciously silent. "Amy, help me," she moaned. "Please."

But instead of jumping to her defense, Amelia crossed her arms over her chest and glared. "Oh, no, Becky. You can handle Lukas on your own. Simon told me what you told him."

As her younger sister continued to glare at her, Rebecca felt her insides twist into knots. "He shouldn't have said anything to you."

"*Nee, you* shouldn't have said anything to *him*."

"Hold on," Lukas interrupted. "What happened with Simon, Amelia?"

Still looking mad enough to spit nails, Amelia said, "Don't worry, Lukas. Nothing happened. Absolutely nothing happened. When he took me out walking the day I got Princess, he told me that it was likely nothing ever would, either."

Now she felt terrible. "I'm sorry, Amelia. I shouldn't have interfered."

"*Nee*, you should not have. So, I wish you well with your romance with Jacob Yoder. But don't expect me to hope that Lukas doesn't interfere." She flounced off into the kitchen.

When Rebecca started after her, Darla placed a hand on her arm. "Leave her be. She's been upset for a couple of days now. She'll be better now."

"I hope so."

"Do I even want to know what was said between Simon, you, and Amelia?" Lukas asked.

Rebecca shook her head. "Probably not."

Lukas groaned. "Why did Levi have to leave me? I'm trying to do my best with you two but it ain't easy."

"Probably because we're adults, Lukas. We don't need you 'doing your best with us,' " Rebecca bit out.

"You should have taken your own advice to heart!" Amelia called out.

"I'm sorry. You're right!" Rebecca said. "I won't interfere again."

"Interfere with what?" Lukas's voice rose. "What is going on with Simon and Amelia?"

"Nothing!" Amelia called out.

Darla held out her hands. "Everyone, calm down. The Yoders will be here any minute."

Just then, there was a knock at the door.

Darla smiled. "It looks like you were saved by the knock, Rebecca."

"And not a moment too soon," she blurted, just as Lukas strode to the door.

Rebecca was really starting to wonder why she thought this dinner party had ever been a good idea.

# Chapter 22

Proving that Lukas could rise to any occasion, he smiled like he didn't have a care in the world when he opened the door. "Good evening," he said easily. *"Wilcom."*

"Good evening to you, Lukas," Mr. Yoder said as he entered, followed by Mrs. Yoder, Lilly, and at last Jacob, who was carrying an enormous basket.

Eager to put her little argument with Lukas behind her, too, Rebecca hugged Lilly and smiled fondly at Jacob.

As Darla led the group into the gathering room, Mrs. Yoder stopped and stared at the table. "Look at the tablecloth! And the fancy glasses and dishes, too! And the flowers in the center! It looks so pretty."

*"Danke,"* Darla said.

"You shouldn't have gone to so much trouble."

Lukas met Rebecca's gaze. "See," he teased. "The girls were busy all afternoon, fixing everything up just right."

"We had fun," Rebecca said.

"I bet," Mrs. Yoder remarked. "It makes me feel special, indeed."

Amelia, Rebecca, and Darla all started laughing at once.

"What's so funny?" Lilly asked.

"Only that this table has been a source of conversation for the last hour," Rebecca explained.

When Lilly still looked confused, her grandmother wrapped an arm around her shoulders. "Come into the kitchen, child. There, I'll tell you all about what getting ready for dinner guests means to men . . . and women. They are two mighty different things, for sure."

At last, Rebecca's spirits lifted. Things might go just fine after all.

WHEN THE MEN were alone, they sat down in the living room and talked about the mill and the latest crops. Oscar waddled in, eyed Jacob's *daed*, then jumped on the couch next to him.

To Jacob's surprise, his father held the puppy with ease, cuddling him close. Jacob was about to say something about how everyone seemed to like puppies when he noticed that Lukas was eyeing him in a completely new way. An almost suspicious way.

"Rebecca was eager for you all to arrive," he said.

"We were looking forward to the meal as well," Jacob said stiffly.

"Huh," Lukas said.

Eager to move the conversation forward, Jacob gestured toward the large fireplace in the center of the room. Its face was made of limestone and its mantel looked to have come from a redwood trunk. It was smooth and gorgeous. A true focal point.

It also looked like it had been in place for decades.

"That's a fine-looking piece of wood," he said. "Redwood?"

His expression relaxing, Lukas nodded. "It is. My grandfather had it shipped out by train almost fifty years ago. The story goes that it took him and three of his friends to wrestle that trunk into his shop and slice it in half. Then weeks to sand and polish it until it was good enough for my grandmother."

"It's big, I'll give you that," Jacob's *daed* said. "I bet your *dawdi* needed half the workers at the mill to cart it in here and put it in place."

Lukas laughed. "Just about."

"Did you grow up in this *haus*, Lukas? Or did your grandparents stay here while you lived elsewhere?" Jacob asked.

"*Nee*, I grew up here. When my mother married, she and Daed elected not to build a *dawdi haus* for my grandparents, even though they said they wouldn't mind moving into one." Looking reflective, Lukas added, "My mother wanted to live close to her parents, and my father, well, he liked my mother happy."

"Sounds like he was a smart man," Jacob's *daed* said.

Lukas grinned. "He was. But I think he enjoyed everyone living under one roof. My siblings and I sure did." Resting his elbows on his knees, he said, "We made a lot of good memories here. Someone was always around and had plans for the rest of us. We were a noisy lot." He paused, then shook his head. "It's hard to believe there are only four of us in the house now."

"More family will come in time," Jacob's father said. "Before you know it, you'll have more feet running down the halls. It's the way of it."

Lukas nodded. "I know you're right. God provides what we need when the time is right."

Until that moment, Jacob had only thought of Lukas as the owner of an extremely successful business. Lukas's admission about all he had lost made him seem more approachable. He was starting to understand Rebecca's loyalty—not just to him but their company, too. The Kinsingers weren't just close; their lives intertwined.

It was so different from his own upbringing. He and Marc had always gotten along, but Jacob had never considered them especially close. But maybe that was his fault? After all, when his parents had yearned to return to Ohio, Marc had gone with them, choosing to live close by, too. Jacob had been the family member who had elected to stay in Florida and work in carpentry. He suddenly wondered if he'd made the wrong choice all those years ago.

"That must be quite a feeling, knowing that you are continuing in your father's footsteps," he said.

To his surprise, instead of nodding, Lukas rubbed a hand along the back of his neck. "To be honest, I don't know if I am following in Daed's footsteps or not. My father was a wonderful man. I am . . . Well, I am simply trying to do my best."

"Your father would've been proud of you," his *daed* said.

Lukas stared at him. "You think so?"

"I know so. Don't forget, I grew up in Charm and knew your father well. You are right, he was a *gut* man. Everyone respected him."

"Truly?"

"Absolutely. Well, except for when we all went fishing together." Shaking his head sadly, Jacob's *daed* said, "I'm sorry to tell ya, son, but your father was a terrible fisherman. Talked nonstop, he did."

Lukas laughed. "You're right. My friend Roman told me that they'd only ask Daed to fish on every other trip."

"That sounds about right," his father said with a grin.

Lukas studied him. "I'm sorry, but I wasn't under the impression that you and Daed had been close. I guess since you didn't work at the mill I figured you two didn't know each other well."

"I never worked for him, but we visited with each other at church for decades." He stretched out his legs. "Church is the great equalizer, *jah*? There, we're all the same in each other's hearts."

"I suspect that is true." Lukas exhaled. "*Danke* for sharing some of your memories with me."

"No need to offer thanks. I miss him, too, son. It brings me pleasure to talk about him."

Looking a bit overcome with emotion, Lukas smiled tightly. Then, with a sigh, he turned to Jacob. "Before we join the women, I'm simply going to ask. Are you courting my sister?"

Jacob didn't know whether to burst out laughing or answer as quickly as possible. He decided on the latter. "I'm hoping to."

"Hoping?"

"Rebecca is a busy gal. I'm trying to wedge myself into her life. At the moment, I'm only getting to walk her places. But I intend to push her a bit."

Lukas looked thoroughly confused. "Why do you want to do such a thing?"

"Have you seen your sister?" his father interjected. "She's a fetching thing."

Jacob groaned. "Daed, stop."

"I don't lie. She's pretty."

"I know that. But that don't mean you need to notice it." Glancing Lukas's way, Jacob said, "I'm sorry. I hold your sister in high esteem. I hope I have your blessing to court her."

Lukas's blue eyes danced. "I, uh, recently became aware that I need to sometimes be my sisters' brother and not makeshift guardian. If Becky means that much to you, I wish you well."

"*Danke.*"

After glancing at the closed kitchen door, Lukas lowered his voice. "And if I could, let me tell you a secret."

"*Jah?*"

"Take her to the pond on the outskirts of our property. It's her favorite spot."

"She's fond of water?"

Lukas winked. "*Nee.* She's fond of turtles."

As luck would have it, all the women came in just then.

Lilly looked the most puzzled. "Who's fond of turtles, Dawdi?"

"Rebecca." Smiling broadly, his father added, "We've had quite a lively discussion out here. All kinds of things are being discussed."

Jacob inwardly groaned. His father couldn't keep a single conversation to himself.

Looking as awkward as Jacob felt, Lukas climbed to his feet. "Before things get any livelier, I think this conversation should move on." Turning to face the women, he said, "Amelia, please tell me that it's time to eat."

"It is, thank goodness. Come to the table everyone."

As they crossed the room to take their seats, Jacob caught up to Rebecca, who looked beyond embarrassed.

Fearing she blamed him for talking about her, he leaned close. "I'm sorry. I don't know how your name came up. But I promise, nothing bad was said. We meant no disrespect."

"I'm certainly not upset with you. Besides, I'm the one who should be apologizing to you, Jacob. Lukas sometimes takes his job as an older brother too seriously."

"He can ask me all the questions he would like. It ain't going to bother me none."

"Why is that?"

"You know why. Because I do want to court you. What's more, I'm planning to tell you that after supper on your front porch."

She giggled. "You're going to take me out to the front porch, just as if we are teenagers?"

"Of course, Becky. Why should they have all the fun?"

She giggled again, just as Lukas scowled over at them. "Are you two going to join us at this fancy setup so we can pray and eat?"

Rebecca tossed her head. "We're on our way, Luke. Settle down."

# Chapter 23

*Monday, September 21*

Jacob considered himself to be a fairly smart man. He also considered himself to be a person who didn't let a good opportunity pass him by. That was why he strode into the main office two days after Lukas had told him about Rebecca's favorite spot.

She was sitting behind her desk, sorting through papers while Simon and a young woman argued with each other and her.

"Mercy, you need to own up to your mistakes," Simon said. "You got my order wrong. Just admit it, then we can move on."

"I didn't make any mistakes. There's nothing to admit."

"Actually, there kind of is," Rebecca interjected. "At the moment, we have three thousand extra three-inch nails."

Simon crossed his arms over his chest. "Which is why Mercy needs to call them up and fix things."

When Mercy raised her chin and looked prepared to plead

her case again, Rebecca said quickly, "It ain't that easy, Simon. They might not accept any returns."

"Then she better get on the phone." He glared at Mercy. "I'm hoping you can handle *that* phone call."

Mercy placed her hands on her hips. "I can handle it just fine. But this ain't my mistake. It's yours, Simon. I said exactly what you told me to say. Either you gave me the wrong number or the distributer sent more than I ordered. It weren't me."

Wearily, Rebecca looked from Simon to Mercy. "Someone needs to get those extra boxes out of Warehouse One. Jackson is going to have a fit when he comes in tomorrow and he can't do inventory."

Simon pointed to the phone. "Then I guess you better handle it."

Jacob had heard enough. Though he was the new guy at Kinsinger's, he'd had a lot of experience working on crews that played pass the buck. He certainly wasn't going to let it play out in front of him at Rebecca's expense.

Stepping forward, he said, "It's five o'clock, Rebecca. Pack up your things, it's time to go."

She blinked at him owlishly. "What?"

"You heard me. You *know* we have plans. Don't make us late."

Simon narrowed his eyes. "Excuse me, uh, Jacob, but we're in the middle of something here."

"Oh?" Keeping his voice firm, he asked, "Do *you* have plans at five o'clock?"

Simon blinked. "Well, *nee.*"

"*Gut*, then you and Mercy can straighten it out. Rebecca is leaving."

Mercy stepped forward, a look of panic in her eyes. "But she handles things like this all the time. Rebecca, can't you—"

"She can't. Plus, she shouldn't have to. I don't know which one of you made the mistake, but it sure wasn't her. Fix it without her."

"I hope wherever you're going is important," Simon said around a sigh.

To Jacob's amusement, Rebecca was already standing up, purse in hand. "I'm sorry. It is. It's terribly important." Looking at both disgruntled parties, she frowned. "*Danke* for taking care of those nails. The invoice with all the phone numbers is right there." Walking to Jacob's side, she smiled. "Sorry to make you wait. I'm ready."

Jacob rested his palm on her back and guided her out of the office. After they'd turned the corner, he couldn't hide his grin. "You did a *gut* job getting out of there."

"Any chance you want to tell me why I just lied to two of my coworkers? Where are we going?"

"Your favorite place."

She stopped. "What place is that?"

"The pond. You, Rebecca Kinsinger, are going to take me to the pond, sit with me on the bank, and show me those turtles."

"That's why you pulled me out of there?"

"I pulled you away because they were taking advantage of you and I got tired of it."

She bit her lip. "I hope Simon and Mercy never find out what we're doing. They would be so mad."

"You can't take on everyone's problems. Not at home or here at work." When she still looked unsure, he gentled his voice. "Remember when you said that you'd like to start thinking more about yourself?"

"I remember," she said softly. Pointing to a small street, she said, "Let's go through here. It's a shortcut."

He slowed his pace and started asking her about the rest of her day. As they walked down the street, turned, then started across a field, she talked. Then she asked him about his day. And then she simply looked at ease.

When the pond was in view, she sighed in contentment. "Here we are."

He reached for her hand. "It's pretty."

"You really think so? Levi always says it's a pretty boring little pond."

Jacob reckoned Levi was right. It was just a little body of water. It wasn't terribly picturesque and neither were the trees that surrounded half of it, but what was mesmerizing was the look of, well, glee on Rebecca's face as they got closer.

"Oh, Jake, look! They're out!" She dropped his hand and rushed forward. Then, like a child, she flopped down on a thick log that someone years ago had rolled on its side and placed next to the water.

"Do you see them? Aren't they adorable?"

Making himself turn away from her, he sat down on the log beside her and looked at the little line of green turtles on a fallen tree branch in the middle of the pond.

There had to be at least ten of them in a row. What was amazing was that they were all facing the same direction. Each one was facing Rebecca. Almost as if they'd been looking for her.

"Do they do this every time you come out?" he asked.

"Do what?"

"Line up and face you?" He held his breath, half waiting for her to chide him. Saying that they were simply sunning.

But instead, she nodded, her blue eyes still glowing like she was witnessing a miracle. "Pretty much."

"I'm glad we came, then," he said softly. Because he was.

He wouldn't have missed this moment for the world.

Because, right at that moment, with ten tiny turtles looking on, he'd just fallen completely, unabashedly, head-over-heels in love.

# Chapter 24

It was only the middle of the afternoon, but Jacob and most of the men on his team had already been working for hours. A builder down in Cincinnati had placed a large order for shells, but needed the job rushed, on account of their better than expected sales.

Marcus, their team leader, had called them all together for an informal meeting two days ago. There, he'd offered a good-natured competition: The man who completed the most shells by the end of the week was going to get a bonus of two hundred dollars. It was a good sum, for sure. But Jacob knew that the amount had been chosen carefully. It was enough to be enticing, but not so grand that any of them would do something foolish in order to attain it.

As Marcus had no doubt anticipated, the tease of that bonus had been all the men needed to work even harder. Though they all talked about the extra money, it was soon apparent that the winner would have bragging rights, which trumped any extra cash in his pocket. The contest had also instigated a certain amount of trash-talk, which made the long hours and sore muscles easier to bear.

"What are ya going to do when I get the bonus, Jacob Yoder?" Samuel called out from his station. "Cry? Or resign yourself to feeling inadequate?"

"You should be asking yourself that," Jacob countered.

"You sound awfully prideful for a man new on the job."

"I may be new, but I'm no stranger to building shells quickly." Looking at the five frames he'd completed since he'd arrived that morning, he gloated. "Maybe when I get the bonus, I'll buy you a ticket to Pinecraft. You can hop on the Pioneer Trails bus."

"You gonna send Sam on vacation?" another man called out.

"No way. I'm gonna send him down to my old crew leader. Justin will teach Samuel a thing or two, and all while the sun is shining on his shoulders and he's sweating like the devil."

Laughter rang out as Samuel said something just bad enough that the men were glad that no women were nearby to hear.

Jacob smiled to himself as he adjusted his protective glasses, turned on the saw, and focused on his work again. Though he missed his brother every day, it was moments like this when he was careful to give thanks to the Lord for creating his silver lining. He loved his new job. Loved it. Ever since he'd started at Kinsinger's, he felt like he'd found a place where he belonged.

Actually, his entire life in Charm was *gut*.

Better than that, even. He was closer to his parents than he'd ever been. Though he'd worried that having supper with them every night might feel confining after years of living his bachelor lifestyle, he soon realized that nothing could be further from the truth. He liked his parents. He liked getting to know them as adults. And he couldn't help enjoy being spoiled a bit. There was something to be said for having a home-cooked meal every evening.

Just as special to his heart was his relationship with Lilly. Watching her come out of her shell was a joy to behold. She smiled more, teased him often, and now hugged her grandparents all the time. He knew their love and patience had made a huge difference in her life, but her happiness at school had also. She loved the new challenges of her schoolwork and was also happy to finally be accepted for who she was.

Lastly, Jacob would be lying if he didn't give Peter quite a bit of credit for her happiness as well. The young man doted on her.

Though Jacob had been taken aback by the idea of Lilly being so close to a boy when she was only thirteen, his parents had taken the development in stride. "Let her be, Jacob," his mother had said. "*Got* placed this boy in her life when she needed someone to trust. Only He knows what will happen in their future, but for now, it is a blessing."

It surely was.

Besides, Jacob knew he wasn't one to talk. He was in his own romantic relationship, and her name was Rebecca. If he had his way, Jacob knew he'd think about her constantly. He couldn't seem to help it. Actually, he didn't even want to try not thinking about her.

Over the years, he'd been attracted to other women. He'd even been smitten with a couple of them. But he had never felt like he did now.

Now he knew what love felt like. He was smitten and captivated. Unsure and tentative, both at the same time. To feel so many emotions, all wrapped around a band of hope? It was a glorious thing.

Smiling to himself, he turned off the table saw and picked up the plank, tilting it right then left, eyeing it carefully. At last he discovered the flaw. One corner hadn't been cut perfectly. It sloped, creating a noticeable bump in its line. The plane of the wood needed to be leveled and the corner adjusted.

Jacob picked up a favorite old tool of his—a narrow blade that he kept deadly sharp. It could cut through the hardest strip of wood like butter. Carefully, he made one minuscule stroke with the hand saw. After the offending portion fell to the floor, he smoothed the plank. Running his hand along the grain, he nodded, then noticed another imperfection. Lifting the blade, he positioned it carefully. With one sharp motion, he began the cut.

Suddenly a loud cry pierced the air. His hand jumped, and right then and there, the blade jumped, too. Instead of slicing through the piece of pine, the sharp blade neatly sliced his forearm.

He dropped the blade with a curse.

Holding up his arm, he stared at it with an increasing sense of detachment. It was a good long cut and bleeding heavily. Drops of blood were staining his skin, soaking into his shirt. It was a real mess. He was going to need stitches. Quite a few of them.

The moment that reality hit him, sharp, stinging pain erupted across his arm. It felt like it was on fire. As the wound continued to bleed, it occurred to him that he should call for help. But when he turned to do that, he suddenly realized that there was another person in the room whose condition was far worse than his own.

Reaching for a rag, Jacob hastily wrapped it around his arm and hurried out of his station, anxious to see how he could be of help. But when he got closer, he drew up short. His pain was forgotten as his mind came to grips with what he was seeing.

Amos was on the ground. He was one of the senior men on their team, though no one he knew would call him old. Jacob reckoned he was around fifty.

Peering through the crowd of men, Jacob noticed that Amos was lying motionless and that the skin around his lips was turning blue.

A few steps away, Marcus was talking into his cell phone. His expression was intense and he kept glancing at Amos, then speaking into the receiver. It was obvious that he was talking to the emergency first responders.

"What happened?" Jacob asked Samuel.

"Not sure."

The door to the warehouse opened and both Lukas and Rebecca Kinsinger came running inside. Right behind them was none other than Peter, whose eyes were fastened on Lukas. It was obvious the boy was completely focused on his boss and ready to assist in any way he could.

"Talk to me, Marcus," Lukas called out.

Marcus passed the phone to Frank, his second-in-command. "That was a dispatcher. Ambulance is on the way." More loudly, he said, "We think Amos suffered a heart attack."

Lukas turned to Peter. "Two things. Go stand outside and direct the ambulance workers to this entrance. Then, as soon as they get here, go to Roman Schrock. Do you remember where he is?"

"Warehouse Two."

"That's right. Go to Roman, ask him to get a driver, then hurry to Amos's farm. Amos's *frau*, Beverly, will need to be brought to the hospital. You understand?"

Peter nodded.

"*Gut*. Now go." Lukas knelt beside Amos.

Jacob noticed most of the other men were like him, trying to see what was going on but staying out of the way. He'd just closed his eyes to say a prayer for Amos when he heard his name being called.

"Jacob! What happened to you?" Rebecca called out.

His eyes popped open. "Hmm?"

She was at his side. "Your arm! Jacob, you're bleeding something awful."

With some bit of shock, he looked down and realized that the rag he'd wrapped around his arm had a sizable red stain on it. "Huh," he said. "I'd forgotten about this."

"Jacob, sit down, man," Samuel said, pressing his shoulders.

Aware that he was about to stumble, Jake did as he was told.

Suddenly feeling a bit foggy, he heard Marcus talking on the phone again. "Looks like we're gonna need another ambulance," he said. "*Jah*," he continued, his voice turning more weary. "*Jah*. Same place. We got a man with a good cut on his arm. It don't look life threatening, but he might need surgery."

*Surgery*? Jacob groaned. This was the last thing his parents and Lilly needed to deal with.

When she heard his groan, Rebecca reached out and pressed a hand to his cheek. "Oh, Jacob, I hope you'll be all right."

He was fine. Well, kind of. "I don't need no ambulance."

Standing over him now, Lukas shook his head. "Don't argue. We don't take chances around here. Not anymore."

Knowing the history, Jacob didn't protest. He merely sat still until sirens were heard and a team of four EMTs arrived with a stretcher, a pack of supplies, and a portable defibrillator.

All the workers watched in respectful silence as they knelt around Amos, who was barely conscious.

Ten minutes later, they were carrying him out. Lukas followed. His voice was clipped and sure as he told the EMTs Amos's full name and age.

Rebecca grabbed Jacob's good hand. "I'm so sorry you got hurt," she whispered as she pressed a fresh cloth someone had handed her to his cut.

"Don't worry. I'll be fine." He attempted to smile and reassure her.

Sirens rang through the air again. Moments later, another team ran in. Immediately, Marcus escorted them to Jacob's side. After motioning Rebecca to move, two men knelt next to him. "What happened?"

"Saw got the best of me. I'll be all right."

"Can you stand up or do you want a stretcher?"

"My arm's hurt, not my feet. I can walk."

Rebecca pressed a hand to his good arm. "Jacob, are you sure?"

There were some things a man had to do. And one of them was walk when he could. Another was not to look weak in front of the woman he loved.

"Don't worry," he said as he climbed to his feet. "Like I said, I'm fine." Feeling more than a little light-headed, he took some time to reassure her. "It's just a cut. I'll be better after a doctor patches me up."

"Grab his arm," one of the EMTs said. "He looks like he's about to go over."

"I'm fine," he said. But the room kept spinning.

Marcus got under his other arm. "If you faint, we're never gonna let you forget it," he said. "Focus."

"I'll follow you to the hospital, Jacob," Rebecca said. Leaning close, she whispered, "Please listen to the doctors. I love you."

Rebecca loved him?

Jacob jerked his head to meet her gaze, realized the motion was too fast, and then slowly came to the conclusion that he was going to get ribbed about his weakness for years. Then he didn't care anymore, because the whole room went black.

# Chapter 25

Jacob was the one who had just gotten carried off in an ambulance, but it was Rebecca who couldn't breathe. She was frozen in the warehouse's doorway, gripping the frame like it was the only thing keeping her upright.

Maybe it was.

"Rebecca? Rebecca, listen to me."

She knew she should answer but couldn't seem to find any words. Instead, she kept her eyes fastened on the EMTs as they loaded Jacob's gurney into the ambulance.

"Rebecca!"

"What?" she blurted, finally realizing that two strong hands were gripping her shoulders hard. "Lukas, that hurts."

Instead of removing his hands, he turned her to face him. His icy blue eyes—the ones he shared with Amelia—looked at her intently. "Becky, get ahold of yourself. We got no time for female dramatics in here."

His tone was less than kind. And, she supposed, completely warranted.

Though she yearned to watch Jacob's ambulance disappear from the property's back entrance, Rebecca forced herself to inhale deeply and then exhale slowly. Her brother was right. She also claimed the Kinsinger name and she wasn't about to put it to shame.

"Sorry, Luke."

"No need for apologies." His tone was far softer now. Far more gentle. Bending so he could stare into her eyes, he said, "Are you better now or do you feel faint? If you're dizzy, grab hold of me. I don't think the men can take the sight of one more person falling to the ground."

He wasn't joking. He really was worried that she was going to collapse on him.

That was all she needed to get her attitude back. "I'm fine now. I promise, I'm not going to faint on you."

Exhaling in relief, he let go of her shoulders at last. "*Gut.* I need you too much for that."

His admission felt good. This was why she'd come back to work. She wanted to be needed. She wanted to feel as much a part of the family business as her brother was. "Are you going to be all right?" she whispered.

"Of course."

Of course. Lukas would say that even if he had been the one with a sliced arm. He simply didn't let himself show weakness to anyone but, she suspected, his wife.

Looking around the warehouse, and at the group of men still standing in pairs looking shocked, he said, "Rebecca, I think I'm going to need to stay here for a little bit. I need to figure out what happened with Amos."

"It was a heart attack, Luke."

"I know it was." Frowning, he continued. "However, he's not that old, and Marcus told me that he couldn't remember Amos ever saying he had heart problems." Rubbing the back of his neck, he said, "Then there's Jacob's accident. He was skilled and came here with a lot of experience. For him to get a cut like that? It don't make sense."

"I understand." For both Lukas's peace of mind and the men's families he needed to understand the cause of both men's emergencies. "What would you like me to do first?"

"I need you to go to the reception area and type up a note for all our workers saying that Amos and Jacob have gone to the hospital. Don't give more details. I don't even want to chance giving out wrong information. Understand?"

"*Jah.*"

"As soon as you get that printed, send Mercy out to deliver that note to every department head." His voice hardened. "Becky, you tell her in no uncertain terms not to stand around and linger and gossip. Everyone needs to know what's going on, but I don't need any silly girl deciding to add her own spin to things."

"I'll do that right now."

"*Danke.* And when the phones start ringing, don't give anyone information who isn't family or an employee."

She shook her head. "I won't."

He snapped his fingers. "As soon as I see Peter, I'm going to send him your way. He needs to go see Jacob's family and tell them what happened. But make sure you have him tell them that it's just a cut. It's a bad one, but he's gonna be all right. We're just being extra careful."

"*Jah,* Lukas," she replied, though a part of her was dismayed. She had hoped to eventually get to Jacob's side at the hospital, but that wasn't going to happen anytime soon.

"*Danke,* Becky." Lowering his voice, he said, "Look, I know you're worried about Jacob. I know you told him that you were gonna go to the hospital." His voice cracked from the strain. "But I can't let you go just yet."

"I understand." That was true. She completely did understand.

He continued as if she hadn't spoken. "I'm real sorry, but with Daed gone and Levi, too . . . I just don't think I can get through these next few hours without you."

"I won't leave you, Lukas."

His eyes watered before blinking it away. He was rattled. No doubt, the sirens had brought back memories of the fire—of losing all those men. Of losing Daed. Rebecca knew how he felt because she felt the same way.

After smiling weakly, she turned toward the front door, just as she heard Lukas say, "Men, I need to know what happened. Marcus, you start."

As she walked the short distance from Warehouse Four to the main office building, Rebecca blinked quickly before she dissolved into tears.

Now she understood why her dream to teach school hadn't come true. Her brother needed her here. Sometimes, only family could make a person feel like everything was going to be okay.

Sometimes only family would do.


RACHEL'S HEART CLENCHED the moment Meghan told her about the two ambulances that were seen at the lumber mill.

"Do ya know what happened there?" she asked, barely able to keep her voice from shaking. "Was . . . Was it another fire?"

The teenager shook her head. "I don't think so, Mrs. Mast. All I heard was that there were two ambulances. No one said a word about fire trucks. There's no smoke, either."

Rachel pressed a hand to her chest. "Oh, of course there isn't." How could she have forgotten the great billowing cloud that had seemed to blanket Charm the day of the fire?

"Your husband works at Kinsinger's doesn't he?"

"*Jah*. He's a team leader in one of the warehouses."

Immediately, Meghan opened her teal backpack and pulled out a cell phone. "Would you like me to call Kinsinger's and ask if your husband is okay?"

She would, but Marcus would be so embarrassed if she asked an English teen to check on him. "*Nee*, but thank you. If every employee's family called up the main office, no one there would get any work done." Attempting to look calmer than she felt, Rachel said, "If something happened to Marcus, the Kinsingers would send someone here to tell me."

"Oh, all right. Can I get Lilly now?"

"Of course." Rachel had kept Lilly and a couple of other students after school to give them some individual attention. Lilly had offered to help them prepare for a spelling bee. Raising her voice, she said, "Lilly, go on out with Meghan and do your studies. The rest of you, get out a sheet of paper. I'll call out some new words for you."

But just minutes after Lilly walked out the door, Rachel spied Peter running toward the schoolhouse. He'd taken the day off to work at the mill.

Not even caring that she was in the middle of a spelling test, Rachel tore open the door and ran out to meet him. "Peter, what happened?"

With obvious reluctance, he turned his attention from Lilly at the picnic table to her. "Hiya, Aunt Rachel. I'm sorry, but I've got to tell Lilly something."

"Is it about the mill?"

"I told them about the ambulances I heard were there," Meghan supplied from Lilly's side.

Peter nodded. In a serious tone, he said, "One man had a heart attack and had to be rushed to the hospital." He inhaled, then said in a rush, "But Lilly, the other ambulance was for your Onkle Jacob."

Rachel's hands shook as she processed that her husband was safe . . . but her poor student was facing yet another crisis.

"What happened?" Lilly's voice was barely a whisper.

"He cut himself."

Tears filled her eyes. "Is . . . Is he gonna be all right?"

Just as Rachel was going to give her a hug, Peter stepped toward the girl. "*Jah*. But your grandparents want you to come home right now. When you get home, they're going to hitch up the buggy and go to the hospital."

Lilly paled. "He needed to go to the hospital?" Lilly glanced Rachel's way. "Mrs. Mast?"

"Of course you can go, dear. Grab whatever you need."

"I'll be right back, Peter," Lilly said.

"I'll drive you both," Meghan interjected. "Then, if you and your grandparents need a ride to the hospital, I can take you there, too."

After swallowing hard, she nodded. "Okay. I'll be right there." Then Lilly darted inside to grab her things.

Noticing that Peter was looking increasingly worried, Rachel attempted to soothe him. "Thank you for coming to get Lilly, Peter. You did a fine job telling her about her uncle. I can see why Mr. Kinsinger says you're such a *gut* employee."

Looking pleased, Peter nodded but didn't say anything. When

Lilly rushed back outside, the three of them started walking to Meghan's car. "*Danke*, Mrs. Mast," Lilly said again.

"I'll be praying for your uncle," Rachel assured her. "Take care."

After quietly sharing with the remaining students inside the classroom that Lilly's uncle had an accident but that everything else was all right, she picked up her clipboard again. "Let's continue our spelling words now. Our next word is *Pennsylvania*."

# Chapter 26

*That same day*

From the moment Peter had come to get Lilly at school, he'd worn a serious and intense expression. He'd been kind and reassuring, yet a little quiet.

He didn't say much when they were in the car with Meghan other than to thank her for the ride. After Meghan parked her car and reassured them that she didn't mind waiting to see what her grandparents wanted to do, Peter walked Lilly into the house.

She followed reluctantly. So many emotions were churning through her, she wasn't quite sure how to deal with it all. She was worried about her uncle, wanted to be brave for her grandparents, and ached to lean on Peter. He had become her best friend. But overriding all of that were the stark memories of running into the hospital after learning about her parents' accident.

She didn't know if she was going to be able to step into another hospital.

After telling her grandparents about the accident, and about Meghan's offer, Peter stood to the side while her grandparents debated about what to do. When they finally decided to accept Meghan's offer, Peter seemed relieved.

Lilly, on the other hand, was filled with dread.

With one last look at Lilly, Peter headed back outside. "I'll tell Meghan to wait for you," he said quietly.

"Wait, don't you want to come to the hospital?" She wasn't sure if she was going to be able to get through her visit without him there. Of course, the moment she asked her question, Lilly felt her cheeks heat in embarrassment. Obviously he didn't want to go sit at the hospital!

But amazingly, he looked as if he completely understood. Gently, he said, "I would go with you if I could, Lilly. But I can't. I promised Mr. Kinsinger that I'd get back to the mill and help out some more."

"Oh. Yes. Of course."

"Tell your uncle that I hope he feels better soon," he said as he turned to leave.

While her grandparents bustled around the kitchen gathering keys and wallets, Lilly knew she should say something to them about how afraid she was to return to the hospital. But how could she burden them with her fears right now?

Instead, she gave in to the impulse and walked back out the door. "Hey, Peter?"

He was already halfway down her driveway. When he heard her voice, he turned around. *"Jah?"*

"Are you . . . I mean, is everything all right?" What she really wanted to ask was if everything was all right between them.

His gaze softened. "I'm fine. It's just hard, you know, delivering news like this. Look, I've got to go, but I'll try to come over later, when you're back from the hospital."

Making a decision, she walked a little farther away from the door. "I won't be going there."

"Why not?"

Hating that her limbs seemed to be trembling, she said, "I don't think I could ever step foot in one of those places again. I hate them."

Walking back toward her, he said, "Lilly, they aren't so bad."

"*Nee*, you don't understand." Though it hurt to relive the memories, she explained. "Peter, I was in a hospital waiting room when a doctor came out to talk to me about my parents. He told me, in front of everyone, that they were dead."

Stepping to her side, he reached out and rubbed her arm. "Nothing like that will happen today. Your uncle ain't gonna die. Mr. Kinsinger was simply being extra careful when he sent Jacob to the hospital. I bet he's going to be ready to leave by the time you get there."

His voice sounded firm and knowledgeable. Comforting.

In the wake of such maturity, she felt silly and childish. But sometimes she felt like she still needed to be childish. "Everything you are saying makes sense. But I . . . I just can't go, Peter. Not this time."

He looked pained. "I hate leaving you, especially if you are going to be waiting here by yourself. But I gotta go."

"I understand."

After giving her a tight smile, he turned and started walking at a good clip.

"Lilly, are you ready?" Mommi called out.

"*Nee*. I'm going to stay here."

Her voice hardened. "Don't you think you need to be there for your uncle?"

"I'm sure that would be best. But I can't go. I want to, but I canna do it, Mommi. I can't go back there." When her grandfather looked about to argue, she blurted, "Dawdi, I'll clean the house and start supper. Just please, don't make me go."

They exchanged glances. But to her surprise, instead of attempting to convince her, her grandfather enfolded her in his arms. "I understand, Lilly. *Jah*, you take care of things here. We'll be back as soon as we can."

Sighing in relief, she walked with them to Meghan's car. "Mommi, Dawdi, this here is Meghan."

"Good to know ya," her grandfather said as he opened the passenger-side door.

Lilly walked back to the front porch and waved good-bye, then went inside to make good on her promise. After fishing around in the refrigerator, she found enough vegetables to make some soup. Getting out her grandmother's favorite wooden cutting board, she started slicing carrots. Anything to keep her mind off the memories.

THE NEXT SEVERAL hours passed for Rebecca as if they had been seconds. The moment she got to her desk, she quickly typed up a note telling the bare minimum about Amos and Jacob. At the bottom of it, she added some lines about how they would do everything possible to update all the workers on Amos's and Jacob's conditions and that she and Lukas would appreciate everyone keeping the men in their prayers. To Rebecca's relief, Mercy had been professional and intent on following Lukas's directives to a T.

Rebecca was fairly sure that Mercy's willingness to comply no doubt had something to do with Rebecca's fierce glares. And likely, her thinly veiled threat that Mercy would lose her job if she didn't take her orders seriously.

Peter, though he was four years younger than Mercy, had reacted like a true adult. He'd barely blinked when Rebecca told him to go to the Yoder house and gently impart the news about Jacob's injury.

Practically the moment after Peter left, the phone started ringing. Then, true to Lukas's prediction, her reception area soon became as busy as the flea market on a Saturday morning. Concerned workers stopped by, anxious for news about Amos and Jacob. Other people called, all wanting information. Most everyone was polite and respectful. Rebecca smoothly handled their myriad concerns as patiently and competently as she could. She also took care to follow Lukas's orders. She gave information as she learned it, sending Mercy back out with new information twice.

The first bit of news was that Jacob Yoder was going to be just fine. His cut had been terrible, for sure. He had needed seventeen stitches. However, the blade hadn't cut anything vital, and that was a blessing. He was still at the hospital, but was expected to be sent home within the hour in the company of his parents.

Amos Taylor had suffered a heart attack. However, it was a relatively minor one. He had survived, was conscious and talking to people, and was currently undergoing tests. An hour after that, Lukas had been told that Amos was expected to be in the hospital for another day at the very least. If the doctors recommended surgery, Amos would be transferred to a different, larger hospital, most likely in Mansfield or Cleveland.

Later, the vans had taken all the Amish workers home, and most of the team leaders had locked their sections of the mill. The reception area had cleared out and the phone had finally stopped ringing. She'd sent both Peter and Mercy home earlier, fervently thanking both for all of their help.

Lukas was still on the phone. However, his tone had lost its staccato rhythm and he was both listening to others with ease and answering with care and patience. She noticed that even the lines of stress around his eyes had softened.

While he finished up his latest call, Rebecca cleaned up her area, then entered his office. When he smiled at her, she sat in one of the chairs directly across from his desk and stretched out her legs. They had done it. They had survived this crisis.

A few minutes later, when Lukas at last hung up, clicking the phone off with a resigned jab, he pressed a palm to his temple and rubbed. "I didn't think I was ever going to get to say good-bye to that man."

"You going to be okay?" she asked.

He said nothing at first. Finally, when he opened his eyes, his gaze was piercing. "*Jah*. You?"

She nodded. "*Jah*. I'm going to be fine, too."

"What a day, huh?"

"Definitely one for the books. We'll be talking about it for years to come."

His lips curved. "Probably." He shook his head. "I'm sorry if I was too curt with you back there in Warehouse Four. I was about to lose it myself."

"You weren't too curt. And even if you were, I can take it."

"*Jah,* you can."

"Hey, were you thinking about the fire, too?"

He looked startled to be asked, then he nodded slowly. "I couldn't help but think about it. There was something about hearing those sirens. In a flash, it all came back. I panicked. I . . . I could feel my heart beating like crazy. And even though everything inside me was telling me that this was nothing like the fire, I felt that same lump lodge in my throat."

"Me, too." If she had been able to put all her jumbled thoughts and feelings into words, she would have said the same exact thing.

"Thanks for getting that note out. I think it prevented a lot of panic."

"Mercy did a good job today."

"I'm glad she didn't tarry."

Rebecca grinned. "I think she was afraid to. I was pretty firm." She decided Lukas didn't need to know about her threats. "I hope you don't mind, but I let Peter leave work an hour early, at four, so Lilly wouldn't be sitting at home alone."

"That was *gut* thinking. Poor thing." Standing up, Lukas said, "I need to go to the hospital and talk to Amos's family. Lock up and then get on out of here, too, okay? I'll see you later."

He looked so alone. "Do you want me to go with you? I don't mind."

"*Danke*, but Darla's going to go with me. She's upstairs in the break room waiting for me. I'll go up and get her."

She was surprised that she hadn't realized Darla had arrived, but then again Darla was very cognizant of Lukas's work. Most likely, she didn't want to be in the way.

"I'm going to go home and see Amelia, then head over to Jacob's *haus*."

"*Gut.*" He was about to turn, but then strode right up and gave her a hug. "Thanks again," he whispered.

Too emotional to do anything but nod, she went to her desk, grabbed her purse, and then left. She needed to get cleaned up and go see Jacob.

She wasn't going to be all right until she saw that he was going to be just fine, too.

# Chapter 27

*That same day*

J ust as she was waving good-bye to her study group, Rachel saw another unexpected guest approaching. But this one was a welcome surprise.

"Marcus!" she cried. Unable to help herself, she rushed down the steps and reached for his hands. "I'm so relieved to see you."

His gaze drifted over her face before he leaned down and pressed a kiss to her brow. "I'm glad to see you, too." Taking her hand, he gently squeezed it. "Are you feeling all right?"

As it always did, the warmth of his touch soothed her like little else could. "I'm better now. But I have to tell ya that things were mighty worrisome for a while. Peter came here to get Lilly. And Meghan told me about the ambulances, too. I was so worried about you."

His eyebrows rose. "About me? Never do that, Rachel. I'm not going anywhere," he said with a hint of a smile.

"Don't act like I'm being foolish. Accidents happen."

"*Jah*, they do," he said as he guided her back inside the building. When they had their privacy, he lightly kissed her lips. "But like I said, I am fine."

"How is Jacob Yoder?"

"He needed a bunch of stitches, but I heard he's going to heal in no time."

"And the man who had the heart attack?"

"It was Amos. Do you remember me speaking of him?"

"*Jah*. His daughter got married last year."

Marcus smiled. "Well, he's hanging in there. Lukas told me that his doctors are going to run some tests to see how his heart is running."

"I'll pray for him, too."

"I know he will be appreciative of that." He stepped back a bit. For the first time since he'd arrived, he looked tentative.

"Is there anything else you wanted to talk to me about?"

"Actually, *jah*."

"What is it?" Rachel braced herself for him to chastise her again about working.

Running a hand along his short beard, he stared at her, then glanced around the room as if he were looking at it for the first time. Rachel looked around, too. She noticed the messy stack of notebooks on one of the side tables. The lessons she hadn't yet erased from the chalkboard. The pile of picture books her youngest pupils had forgotten to put away.

She became aware of the scent of crayons and glue and peanut butter and, well, children. It wasn't unpleasant; no, it was so very familiar to her it made her heart warm. But she was sure that to Marcus this place looked unkempt and disorganized.

"Rachel, as I was walking over, I realized something." He looked up, took a breath, then met her gaze again. "I realized that I was glad you weren't sitting home alone by yourself. I was happy that you weren't pacing our hallway, waiting and wondering how I was doing."

He knew her so well. "You're right. I would have been pacing nonstop."

Instead of smiling at the image, he looked even more determined. "The truth is, though a lot of my friends' wives enjoy the solitude at home, I know that ain't you. I . . . well, after everything that happened today, I realized that I was glad you were working here."

"I don't understand."

"Being here makes you happy. It keeps you occupied. This classroom and the *kinner* you teach are as much a part of your life as Kinsinger's is to me. Ain't so?"

She curved her hands around her middle protectively. "*Jah.* When I am around my little scholars, I feel needed and helpful. Their innocent comments make me smile, their silly antics make me laugh. I feel . . . well, I feel like I am helping these children find their way through life. I love them. Every one of their accomplishments makes me feel worthy—even when Toby learned to tie his laces yesterday."

He smiled. "I'm sorry that I didn't understand that before now."

"When the babe comes, I will stop teaching, Marcus. But for now, I want to be here. Just like you with all the men who work on your team, I have people here who count on me." She smiled slightly. "They may be small, but their needs are just as important."

"Will you forgive me for being so bossy and obstinate?"

Just to tease him, she rolled her eyes. "Ain't that what I always do?"

He grinned. "Careful, Mrs. Mast. I ain't one of your *little scholars.*"

Holding out her hand, she smiled. "No, you are not. You're someone even better. You're my husband. Are you ready to go home?"

"What about your classroom? Don't you need to clean it up or something?"

She did. Of course she did. But some things were far more important than scattered books and ungraded papers. "I think I'll tackle it all tomorrow. Right now, I'd rather walk home with you and count my blessings."

"Lead the way, then, Rachel. You lead and I will follow."

As she picked up her purse and pulled out the keys to lock the door, Rachel decided that sweeter words had never been said.

LILLY HAD WORKED hard on the house while her grandparents were at the hospital. She'd put fresh sheets on her uncle's bed, finished making chicken soup, and baked buttermilk biscuits.

After that, she'd gone to the barn, checked for eggs, and washed the four she found before setting them neatly in the refrigerator.

Then, at long last, Uncle Jacob came home.

Unable to stop her tears, she'd hugged him tight. He'd hugged her back, kissed her brow, and then assured her he was not too worse for wear. Only when her tears were dry did he disappear into the house behind Mommi and Dawdi.

Not too long after that, Peter returned.

She had been sitting on the front porch, simply enjoying the quiet. When he saw her, he smiled. "Hey."

"Hi. How are things at the mill?"

"Good enough. How's your uncle?"

"He's got a big bandage on his arm but he's all right, I guess. He's inside with my grandparents."

"Can I sit with you on the swing?"

Feeling a little awkward, she scooted over and bit her lip when he settled right next to her. "I'm so tired," he said sheepishly. "I feel like I've run all over Charm today."

"You might have." Shyly, she added, "What you did, running out to school to see me? It was a good thing. I'm glad you were the person to tell me about Uncle Jacob."

"Me, too."

After a little while, Peter stretched and placed his arm around her shoulders. Lilly stiffened, unsure what she thought about that, then decided his arm felt comforting. He was warm and steady and smelled good, too.

Because she couldn't think of anything to say, she simply relaxed against him.

Peter seemed to feel the same way. He rocked them back and forth with one foot. Together, they watched the sun glide across the horizon, turning the sky into a pretty mixture of pink and orange before it faded.

Realizing it was going to be dark soon, Lilly turned her head. "Are you sure your parents aren't gonna mind you being over here? It's getting late."

"I stopped home before I came back here. They'd heard about Amos and Jacob. After I filled them in, I told them that I needed to see you. They understood."

"That's nice of them." She smiled shakily.

"I've got nice parents," he said easily. "They understand most things."

"I guess so."

Peter's foot continued to move their swing back and forth. The motion made her slide closer to him. He seemed not to notice that, because he started talking again. His tone was smooth and lazy. The way it usually was. "Lilly, you might not realize this, but until about a year ago, I was kind of a handful."

She had heard rumors about him. Katie had said that he'd been a little wild. Lilly hadn't been all that surprised. Peter seemed to be the type of boy to push boundaries.

"Is that right? What did you do?" she teased. "Did you stay out too late playing and talk back to adults?"

Their *rumspringa* hadn't started yet, of course, but even during their running-around time, most just talked a big game. Hardly anyone ever did anything all that shocking. She sure wasn't planning to.

He laughed. "You should be a detective."

"Not so much. It's just that kids talk. You are a favorite topic, you know."

He rolled his eyes. "People just like to gossip."

"Katie stopped by after you and my grandparents left. She told me she'd heard from her cousin that Mr. Kinsinger had barked orders to you today and that you handled everything like you'd been working there for years."

"I didn't have much of a choice. He was pretty scary. Usually he talks slower and jokes a bit. But he was telling me so many things I had to listen to him and then go do what he asked. Immediately."

"I would have been scared when they took that man away on a stretcher."

"It was scary. All the men in that warehouse looked shaken up." He squeezed her shoulder. "But you don't need to worry about it none, Lilly. It's all over now."

"I'm glad."

"Me, too." He dropped his arm and moved a bit apart from her.

She missed the comfort of his arm around her. She missed his warmth, too. But, of course, what they had been doing wasn't seemly.

"Hey, Lilly?"

"Hmm?"

"Do you want to go for a walk with me?"

"Now? It's getting dark."

He looked at the horizon. "The sun is setting but we've got time. Plus it's a full moon. Want to go? I won't take you far."

"Why do you want to go for a walk?" She'd been having a mighty nice time simply sitting on the swing with his arm around her.

"No reason." But the look he gave her told a different story. Almost as if his reason wasn't all that sweet. Or good.

She wondered what he had in mind. All she knew was that she wanted to find out.

"Let me go tell my grandparents," she said. "I'll be right back."

She hurried inside and found her grandparents sitting in the kitchen with Jacob. They had their hands around big coffee mugs. Uncle Jacob was eating her soup and had a plate of biscuits in front of him.

"Everything okay, Lilly?" Mommi asked.

"*Jah*. Um, Peter asked if we could go for a walk. Do you mind?"

Her grandfather's eyebrows rose. "Now? Isn't it time he went home?"

"We won't be gone long. Please?"

Uncle Jacob said nothing, just looked down at his plate and smiled.

"I don't mind, dear," Mommi said at last. "But you be home in thirty minutes."

*"Danke."* She smiled and ran back outside. "Peter, they said they didn't mind but I have to be back in a half an hour."

He smiled. "Let's go then."

Walking by his side, they strolled toward the barn, walked around it, then headed down a sloping hill toward a thicket of raspberry bushes. Crickets chirped around them. In the distance, near their small creek, Lilly could hear the croak of a bullfrog.

After glancing back at the house, Peter stopped. Then, to her surprise, he held out his arms. "Lilly, come here."

Feeling a little afraid but trusting him, too, she did as she was asked.

The next thing she knew, he was holding her close. "This was what I wanted to do when I came by earlier today," he murmured. "It was so hard to keep my promise to Mr. Kinsinger and only deliver my news, and then leave. I wanted to stay and make sure you were all right."

"I'm all right now." She rested her head on Peter's chest, closed her eyes, and held on. Somehow, he'd known exactly what she'd needed, yet again.

And in doing so, he'd changed a bad day into a good one. One of the best.

# Chapter 28

Rebecca arrived just moments after Lilly came inside from her walk with Peter. After Rebecca said hello to everyone, Lilly and Jacob's parents had gone to their rooms.

It wasn't that late, but it had been a stressful day. Still, Jacob knew that sleeping was the last thing he wanted to do. He felt keyed up and restless.

And Rebecca's last words to him before he'd collapsed still rang in his ears.

She loved him.

Now that they were alone, a new tension existed between them. Rebecca seemed a little awkward, a little hesitant. He suspected she was thinking about her declaration, too.

After he got settled on the sofa, she sat next to him, sitting so that her knees were touching his. He was pleased with their arrangement. He wanted her close enough to see her pretty blue eyes.

She, on the other hand, was staring at his arm. "Oh, Jacob, it looks worse close up."

He chuckled. "You can't see anything, Becky. It's all covered up with bandages."

"*Jah*, but that is a big bandage. You're covered all the way from your wrist to elbow."

He looked down at the white gauze and grimaced. "It looks worse than it feels," he reassured her. Of course, that was no doubt because he had been sent home with some prescription pain-killers. Once the shock had worn off, his "little" cut had actually hurt pretty badly.

"You are lucky that blade didn't cut anything too important."

She was right about that. The doctors had said that if the slice had been just a few millimeters to the right he would have cut one of his veins. But that said, he still felt foolish. "I shouldn't have cut myself in the first place. It was a stupid mistake."

"Don't be so hard on yourself. Accidents happen. It's a fact of lumber mills."

"I agree. But I've been handling saws and knives since I was younger than Peter. This is the worst nick I've ever gotten."

Reaching out, she ran a finger down along his knuckles. Her touch felt cool and soft. "A cut requiring seventeen stitches ain't a nick. You have an injury."

"It's just a cut." Seeking to remove the worry from her eyes, he said, "All the guys in my crew are going to bring this up for the next ten years." He rolled his eyes. "That, and the fact that I went and fainted like a girl."

He still couldn't believe he'd let a little bit of blood—and the sweet declaration from the woman he loved—get to him so badly.

"Hey," she said. "Don't you go start talking bad about girls. After all, no girl fainted today."

He chuckled. "Point taken."

As she continued to caress the hand of his wounded arm, he

reached out with his other hand and linked their fingers. He liked touching her. He liked that she cared about him. Liked how she smelled good and was so pretty. Most of all, he liked how she was currently smiling at him.

"Did I say something else amusing that I wasn't aware of?" he asked.

"It wasn't amusing. But you did say something that made me happy."

"What was that?" So far, all they'd talked about was his injury and the poor way he reacted to it.

"You said that the men would no doubt be teasing you for ten years."

"*Jah?* So?"

Her blue eyes sparkled. "Well, I took that to mean that you plan to be at Kinsinger's for a long time."

This was the perfect time to tell her how he felt. To tell her that he loved her, too.

But instead of blurting all that out, he simply rubbed her hand some more. "I hope I will be at Kinsinger's for years," he said, doing his best to act as if it was the job that meant so much to him. "I mean, as long as your brother and Marcus give me a chance to redeem myself."

"Redeem yourself? Why?"

"I cut myself while another guy was having a heart attack. They had to order an ambulance for me. That's expensive. They may decide that I am too much trouble."

"Lukas was worried about you. He wasn't complaining." She lifted a shoulder. "Besides," she added quietly, "he knows that you and I have grown close."

"We have." Now, at last, it was time. "Rebecca, you have to

know something. I heard what you said to me today. I heard you say that you love me."

Her cheeks bloomed. "Oh." After taking a breath, she continued, each word tumbling over the next. "Well, you see, I was anxious about you—"

He shook his head. "No, you can't take it back."

Her mouth snapped shut. "Why not?"

"Because I've fallen in love with you, too."

She swallowed. For once, it seemed Rebecca Kinsinger, the woman who commented on just about anything . . . was at a loss for words.

It was too cute.

Leaning forward, he brushed a kiss to her temple, then gave in to temptation and let his lips drift along her cheek. When she shivered in response and placed her hands on his chest, he gently pressed his lips to hers. Then he leaned back and held her hands to his chest with one hand. She looked a little dreamy. So very sweet.

And that, it seemed, made the words come easier.

"Rebecca, since I've known you, we've had lots of conversations about dreams and jobs and relatives and what that all means to us. But I don't know if I've ever truly shared with you about how I once had another dream."

"What was that?"

"I wanted a family. I wanted a woman to call my own. A wife. I wanted a partner to go through life with. I've been trying to be the person I thought my parents had always wanted me to be, but then I realized that I've already accomplished something pretty amazing."

She blinked. "What did you do?"

"I found you."

Her hands were shaking as she pulled them away from his chest and placed them on her face. After taking another ragged breath, she clasped her hands tight in her lap.

He pressed on. "Becky, I've come to realize that my life isn't going to be about careers and financial success. It's going to be about waking up in the morning content. It's going to be about going to sleep happy with the person I am sleeping beside. It's going to be about creating a life with someone I love."

After eyeing the empty doorway, Jacob lifted his bandaged arm to rest on the back of the couch, then shifted. With his good arm, he carefully pulled Rebecca close. So close, she was practically sitting in his lap.

Heat filled her gaze before a fierce blush stained her cheeks. "Jacob, stop!" she said in a whispered shriek. "Your parents are going to be shocked."

"I'm thirty years old, Bec. I don't think they're going to be *that* shocked."

"They'll think something has come over you."

But he noticed that she wasn't moving away. Instead, her hands were resting on his shoulders and her eyes were sparkling.

Just to keep them that way, he teased her. "If they ask what's come over me, I'll tell them it's the pain-killers."

"What about me? I haven't taken any drugs. They'll think I'm a floozy," she protested. Still, she didn't back away.

"I'll tell them you are feeling sorry for me." He grinned. "Just stay here a few minutes longer, wouldja, Becky? It's nice to feel you in my arms. Now, tell me you love me again."

"Do you need to hear it? You said you heard me the first time." She smiled coyly.

"*Jah*, but I wouldn't mind hearing it again."

"All right, then." Her eyes met his. "Jacob Yoder, I love you."

"I love you, too, Rebecca. Forever."

"Forever," Rebecca agreed. "And always," she whispered as she cuddled closer.

The feel of her body nestled close made Jacob realize that what they'd shared was exactly right. Perfect, in fact.

Work was good. Family was even more important. But having a person to share both with? To plan a future with? Having the chance to hold a pretty woman in his arms and know that she was everything he'd ever hoped for?

Well, that was truly a dream come true.

## About the author

## About the book

Insights,
Interviews
& More . . .

## Read on

# Meet
# Shelley Shepard Gray

PEOPLE OFTEN ASK how I started writing. Some believe I've been a writer all my life; others ask if I've always felt I had a story I needed to tell. I'm afraid my reasons couldn't be more different. See, I started writing one day because I didn't have anything to read.

I've always loved to read. I was the girl in the back of the classroom with her nose in a book, the mom who kept a couple of novels in her car to read during soccer practice, the person who made weekly visits to the bookstore and the library.

Back when I taught elementary school, I used to read during my lunch breaks. One day, when I realized I'd forgotten to bring something to read, I turned on my computer and took a leap of faith. Feeling a little like I was doing something wrong, I typed those first words: *Chapter One.*

I didn't start writing with the intention of publishing a book. Actually, I just wrote for myself.

The New Studio

For the most part, I still write for myself, which is why, I think, I'm able to write so much. I write books that I'd like to read. Books that I would have liked to have had in my old teacher tote bag. I'm always relieved and surprised and so happy when other people want to read my books, too!

Another question I'm often asked is why I choose to write inspirational fiction. Maybe at first glance, it does seem surprising. I'm not the type of person who usually talks about my faith in the line at the grocery store or when I'm out to lunch with friends. For me, my faith has always felt like more of a private thing. I feel that I'm still on my faith journey—still learning and studying God's word.

And that, I think, is why writing inspirational fiction is such a good fit for me. I enjoy writing about characters who happen to be in the middle of their faith journeys, too. They're not perfect, and they don't always make the right decisions. Sometimes they make mistakes, and sometimes they do something they're proud of. They're characters who are a lot like me.

Only God knows what else He has in store for me. He's given me the will and the ability to write stories to glorify Him. He's put many people in my life who are supportive and caring. I feel blessed and thankful . . . and excited to see what will happen next! ～

# Letter from the Author

Dear Reader,

A funny thing happened in the middle of the editing process for this novel—I was able to go to the photo shoot for the book's cover!

This was an exciting event for me. I had cut out photos for all the characters in the series from magazines and taped them in a notebook. When I began writing the first book in the series, *A Son's Vow*, each character slowly began to come to life. Before I knew it, I had all kinds of scribbled notes about each character. Some were descriptive, like Darla's petite frame, while other notes were more about each character's personality, such as Rebecca's fondness for turtles.

Then one day out of the blue, I was invited to help choose models for the cover of *A Daughter's Dream*. When I clicked through various photos from the modeling agency, I found Jacob and Rebecca easily. Soon after that, I learned that I could actually visit the cover shoot!

A couple of weeks later, my girlfriend Maggie and I were in Michigan. We met Laura, the photographer and designer; Andrea, the makeup artist; and Abby and Steve, the models who would be my characters on the cover. Each person couldn't have been nicer. When I saw Abby, tears filled my eyes. There, sitting right in front of me, was Rebecca Kinsinger! It was really the strangest thing.

I should share that I promised everyone that I wouldn't get in the way. I was fully prepared to stand in a corner and just watch. But to my amazement, Laura asked me for my opinion about the models' clothes. Then she asked me to tell the models about their characters. Abby and Steve smiled when I told them about Rebecca and Jacob. They looked eager to try their hand at being Amish cover models!

Next thing I knew, we were all wandering through fields. Laura took lots and lots of pictures. I did my best to stay out of the way while Andrea continually fixed the folds and tucks on Abby's dress. Immediately, Abby and Steve proved why they were such successful models. They played their parts, smiled and looked reflective, and somehow managed to look comfortable even though the temperature was in the forties and neither was wearing a coat.

As I watched all of this taking place, I felt as if I were actually seeing my characters come to life! By the time I headed back to Cincinnati, I had vowed to myself to go back through the book and make it better. I wanted my story to do justice to the photographer's and models' wonderful work.

Honestly, I don't know if I did that or not. All I do know is that visiting the cover shoot was certainly a dream come true for me! I will be forever grateful to Laura Klynstra for allowing me to join her and to my editor, Chelsey Emmelhainz, who so kindly made it all happen.

I hope you liked the book. I hope you were as delighted with the cover as I was!

Thank you for picking up *A Daughter's Dream*. Thank you for telling your friends and family about it, and for asking your local librarian to carry the book, too.

But most of all, I want to thank you for your support over the years. It's because of you that so many people at HarperCollins work so hard to make these books the best that they can be.

With blessings,<br>Shelley

P.S. If you have time, please tell me what you thought about the book and the cover! You can find me at my website, on Facebook, or on Twitter. You can also write me at the following address: Shelley Shepard Gray, 10663 Loveland Madeira Rd. #167, Loveland, OH 45140.

# Questions for Discussion

1. What does the following scripture verse from Ezra mean to you? *Be of good courage and do it* (Ezra 10:4).

2. Has there ever been an instance in your life when the following Amish proverb would have seemed particularly meaningful? *If we fill our houses with regrets of yesterday and worries of tomorrow, we have no today for which to be thankful.*

3. During the novel, Jacob relies on his parents' advice to help parent Lilly. Who do you go to for advice? Your parents? Spouse? Friends? Why?

4. What do you think of Rachel's dilemma? What about her husband's reaction to her wanting to continue to teach school?

5. One of the themes in the novel centers on dreams that don't come true. Do you think this is a theme that many people can relate to? Why or why not?

6. Lilly's story line continues in the next book, *A Sister's Wish*. What do you think will happen to her next?

7. Jacob returns home after living apart from his family for the last decade. What do you think about his decision to give up his job and life in Pinecraft in order to help his parents and niece? What obstacles do you think he will face?

8. Each member of the Kinsinger family has been dealing with their father's death and the fire at the lumber mill in different ways. What has helped you survive a difficult loss?

9. Jacob and Rebecca have fairly similar personalities. What similar character traits do you share with important people in your life?

10. What do you think is going to happen when Levi eventually returns? ◠

# Granola Bars

1½ pounds miniature marshmallows
½ cup butter
¼ cup vegetable oil
½ cup honey
½ cup peanut butter
1 cup graham crackers (crushed fine)
9½ cups Rice Krispies
5 cups quick oatmeal
1½ cups M&M's
1 cup chocolate chips

Melt together butter and marshmallows in a small saucepan over low heat. Combine rest of the ingredients in a large bowl, then stir in melted marshmallow mixture until combined. Press into baking pans and leave out at room temperature. When cool, cut into squares and serve. ∾

Taken from *Country Blessings Cookbook* by Clara Coblentz. Used by permission of the Shrock's Homestead, 9943 Copperhead Rd. N.W., Sugarcreek, OH 44681.

# A Few *Charming* Facts from Shelley Shepard Gray

1. Charm is located in the heart of Holmes County, Ohio, home to the largest Amish and Mennonite population in the world.

2. The actual population of Charm is only 110 people.

3. One of the public schools in Charm is actually called "Charm School."

4. Charm was founded in 1886. It was once called Stevenson, in honor of a local Amish man, Stephan Yoder and his son.

5. Charm also has a nickname that some locals still use. The name is "Putschtown," which is derived from the word *putschka*, meaning "small clump."

6. The annual "Charm Days" festival is held in the fall every year. The highlight of the festival is the "Wooly Worm Derby."

7. The largest business in Charm is Keim Lumber Company. Located on State Route 557, it has a large retail showroom and website and is open to the public. ❧

# A Sneak Peek
## from the Next Book in the Charmed Amish Life Series, *A Sister's Wish*

*Coming September 2016 from Avon Inspire*

### *Thursday, October 1*

"Princess, *nee*!" Amelia shouted as she scrambled down the front steps. "Stop!"

But Princess didn't listen. Actually, that probably wasn't true. Princess no doubt listened just fine. She simply didn't care to pay much attention to what Amelia wanted her to do.

Instead, the six-month-old pygmy goat continued to nonchalantly chew Oscar's leash.

From what Amelia could tell, the goat had been munching on it for some time. A good section of it was missing.

Thank heavens her sister Rebecca's bulldog puppy was unaware that he was free. Instead of running off as most dogs were wont to do, he was plopped on his side, enjoying the unexpected warmth of the October sun.

After picking up the pup—who at thirty pounds was now really too big to carry—and depositing him inside the screen door of the house, Amelia braced herself. It was time to convince Princess that she really, really needed to listen.

Her pet had a silky white coat, long eyelashes, and beady black eyes. Princess was pretty, smart, and could climb almost anything. She was also as ornery as one might expect of a young doe.

Everyone had warned Amelia about this. Her siblings had begged her to return Princess to the farm where she'd bought her, saying that none of them had time to properly train the animal.

But Amelia had steadfastly ignored both

the warnings and the entreaties. She'd wanted this goat. Actually, she had wanted something to call her own, and a goat would do.

It seemed she was as stubborn as her pet.

"You silly girl," Amelia said. "Rope ain't *gut* for you. You must learn to leave it alone."

Princess bleated in reply.

Unable to help herself, she laughed. "*Jah*, that is what I thought you might say." After carefully pulling the last bit of rope out of Princess's mouth, Amelia wrapped an arm around the pesky animal's neck and guided her to the barn. "Lucky for you I just put some fresh alfalfa in your stall. You can get your fill of that while I do my chores."

Just as she was about to step inside her cozy stall, however, Princess balked. With a grunt and a bleat, she pulled away.

"Princess, I ain't got time for this. It's already two in the afternoon. I need to work on supper." And the garden. And sweep the floors. All the chores that were up to her to complete since she was the lone member of her household working at home.

Really wishing that she'd put a harness or collar on her little goat, Amelia grabbed Princess around the middle and pulled her forward.

But the doe froze, looked panicked, and bleated loudly.

Frustrated beyond measure, Amelia pulled harder. "Come now. I know you are stubborn, but you must start listening to me!"

Princess curled her lips, revealing lots of sharp, shiny white teeth.

Amelia glared right back. "What has gotten into you?" Stepping into the stall, she yanked on Princess again.

"*Bleat!*"

Princess protested frantically, and then kicked out her back legs, just like a donkey.

One tiny, surprisingly sharp hoof made contact with Amelia's shin.

More surprised than anything, Amelia threw her hands up in the air as she fell to the floor of the stall. And when she flung out her hand ▶

## A Sneak Peek (continued)

to catch herself, she discovered why Princess had not wanted to be anywhere near her home.

Because Amelia's left hand landed on a snake.

It didn't take kindly to the interruption. It slithered, hissed, and bit her hand.

Amelia cried out.

Princess scrambled farther away.

Fighting pain in both her palm and leg, Amelia gathered her wits, hobbled out of the stall, and at last leaned back against the wooden enclosure. Then she promptly did exactly what she'd hoped she'd never do . . .

She burst into tears. Terrible, loud, unapologetic tears. She was alone, she was in pain, and suddenly, she'd had enough. More than enough.

Amelia Kinsinger cried for her mother, who'd died when Amelia was only seven. She cried for her father who'd perished in a fire in her family's lumber mill. She cried for her brother Levi who had left to find out more about himself, though none of them had any idea about what he'd hoped to discover.

In short, she cried for everything she'd ever lost and everything she still had.

But most of all, she cried because there was currently no one around to care.

Simon Hochstetler knew Lukas didn't want him calling on his little sister. For most of his life he'd honored his best friend's wishes. But about four months ago, Simon had decided he was tired of waiting.

He was twenty-eight years old, a manager at Kinsinger Lumber and had more than thirty men reporting to him. More important, he'd been in love with Amelia Kinsinger for years. He'd kept his distance out of respect for both her age and the fact that she was his best friend's little sister. But when he had begun to suspect that Amelia returned his feelings, Simon knew something had to change.

And because he'd rarely been the type of man to wait when he wanted something badly enough, Simon had found a way to see Amelia.

He visited her when no one else was around.

He wasn't proud of this. If Amelia's parents had been alive, he would have done whatever it took to persuade them to accept him as a prospective suitor.

But they had both gone up to Heaven and there was no way he was going to beg and plead his case to his childhood friend or Amelia's sister, Rebecca. Amelia was twenty-two and fully able to tell him if she didn't want him around. So far, she'd been delighted by his visits.

So he'd continued to see her on the sly. He'd told himself it was because she needed the company. But the truth was that Simon simply needed her. Amelia was sweet, kind, and honest. She was beautiful, too. She was actually everything he'd ever wanted. More than he'd ever dared to yearn for.

Being in her company made him forget the mistakes he'd made. Her smiles gave him hope, and her acceptance made him feel clean and worthy. There was no way he was ever going to give that up without a fight.

So even though he didn't mind doing whatever it took to see her, Simon knew that wasn't fair to Amelia. It was time to bring their relationship out into the open.

He was practicing different ways to try to convince Lukas of this when he arrived at the Kinsingers' front walkway. Then just as he was about to walk up the front steps, he realized that something wasn't quite right. It was too quiet, unnaturally still.

It was unexpected, too. They'd had plans. Just yesterday he'd asked if she would be willing for him to spend an hour with her. She'd smiled and nodded.

Every other time, she would be outside on the front porch with two Mason jars of iced tea or lemonade, waiting for him.

But Amelia was nowhere in sight. In addition, the front door was open. Only their ratty-looking screen door was preventing Oscar from getting out.

Rebecca's normally lazy pup was staring at him in a pitiful way when he walked up the brick walkway in the front of the house. He whined and pawed at the screen. "Hey, boy," he murmured. "What's going on here?"

Oscar gazed up at him with sad eyes and whined some more.

Simon was growing more concerned by the minute.

"Amelia?" he called out as he trotted up the steps.

She didn't answer.

Opening the screen door, he let Oscar waddle through, then followed him down the steps.

Immediately Oscar did his business. Then, with a little grunt, he trotted toward the barn as quickly as his stocky legs could take him.

His heart in his throat, Simon followed on his heels.

"Amelia?" he called out again.

At last, he heard a gasp, followed by a small cry.

He picked up his pace, dust flying up around his thick work boots. "Amelia, where are ya?"

"I'm . . . I'm in the barn."

Her voice didn't sound right. Running now, he followed the pup inside, then froze at the sight before him.

Amelia was sitting on the dirt floor of the barn crying. Her light pink dress was wrinkled and dusty. Her usually carefully pressed white *kapp* was smudged with dirt.

Even in the dim light he could see that her cheeks were deathly pale, her nose and eyes were red from crying, and she was holding one hand awkwardly in the other. ▶

## A Sneak Peek *(continued)*

After crossing the small space in two strong strides, he knelt by her side. "Amelia, what happened?" He didn't even bother with asking if she was all right. She so obviously wasn't.

She hiccuped. "There was a snake in Princess's stall." She waved her hand. "It . . . it bit my hand."

Simon was barely able to push aside his panic as he reached for her hand. Only the experiences of his past allowed him to control the panic that he was feeling. "Are you sure? Was it a rattler? How long ago did this happen?"

"An hour ago. Maybe a little longer? I'm not sure," she said, answering his last question first. Gazing at her hand that was now firmly held in his own, she visibly gathered herself together. "It was a rat snake, I think. Nothing poisonous, at least, I'm fairly sure about that. But, Simon, it still hurts terribly."

Feeling marginally better, Simon forced his body to relax. If a copperhead or rattler had bitten her, she would likely be much worse off.

But that didn't mean he didn't feel for her. Snake bites, venomous or not, were scary experiences. "I reckon it does." Turning her hand, he searched for the puncture wounds. They were located at the bottom of her palm, less than an inch from her wrist. The affected area was slightly swollen and red. Most of the skin around it looked angry. Even if the snake hadn't been poisonous, he knew the bite should probably be checked out.

"Let's get you on the porch. Once you get settled, I'll hitch up Stormy to the buggy. We'll run over to the emergency clinic."

When she looked up at him with a fierce expression, he braced himself for an argument. Amy was proud, and she hated for people to coddle her. Furthermore, she seemed to be under the misconception that she didn't do enough to garner any concessions.

Ever since her father's death in the fire at the mill and Lukas had taken over the day-to-day operations, she'd seemed intent to do everything at home without complaint or help.

Even though Lukas's new wife, Darla, helped and so did Rebecca, a few hours every now and then didn't make up for the fact that it was Amelia alone who tended the animals, cared for the garden, cleaned the house, did the laundry, and cooked supper every single day.

But to his surprise, instead of arguing, Amelia nodded.

Unable to help himself, he brushed her cheek with the side of his thumb. "I'm glad you understand," he said gently. "Now, give me your hand and I'll help you up."

But when she tried to move, she winced, then cried out.

He froze. "What's wrong?"

Averting her face, she started crying again. Quiet, thick tears that cascaded down her cheeks and broke his heart.

Concerned, he crouched by her side. And promptly forgot all his intentions of treating her in a calm, friendly way. Sidling closer, he wrapped an arm around her shoulders. "Amy, honey? Talk to me, *jah*?"

After taking a fortifying breath, she nodded. "Something else happened, Simon. Princess got scared of the snake and she kicked my shin. It hurts something awful. E-even worse than my hand. I don't know if I can put any weight on it."

With effort, he refrained from reacting. The last thing she needed was for him to either get upset about her injuries or say what was at the center of his mind—that he'd known it hadn't been safe for her to be alone on the farm for hours at a time, day after day.

But of course, casting blame wouldn't help her feel better. "Which leg did she kick?"

Awkwardly, she pointed to the one stretched out. "That one."

The hem of her dress was resting about mid-calf. He lifted the fabric to her knee. ▶

Not seeing anything from that angle, he started to turn her calf when she cried out.

Growing alarmed, he moved to her other side so he could see the full extent of the injury. A large—very large—black and blue mark decorated her leg. It was also extremely swollen and slightly misshapen.

He would bet money that the bone was broken. Visions of her sitting in pain while on the floor of the dusty barn cut him deeply.

Once again, he ached to corner Lukas, Rebecca, and the missing Levi and give them a piece of his mind. Yes, Amelia was an adult, but she had been given too few choices. While the three of them spent their days how they wanted to, Amelia was stuck at home alone day after day.

He'd told Lukas more than once that he worried that something would happen to Amelia and she would be alone and helpless.

He wasn't exactly happy to be proven right.

But none of that mattered now. All that mattered was taking care of Amelia and getting her help as soon as possible.

"Change of plans," he said as he pulled out his cell phone. "We need to get you to the hospital."

The skin around her mouth whitened. "Do ya really think that is necessary?"

"I'm afraid so. I think your leg is broken."

After staring at him for a few seconds, she sighed. "I'm afraid it is, too," she whispered. "I tried to get up but I couldn't put any weight on it."

After pausing for a moment to give thanks that the bishop had allowed him to purchase a cell phone for work, he dialed 911. He'd deal with the consequences of using the phone for a nonrelated work reason at a later date.

He had to walk out the barn door to get a signal, but God was good. In no time at all, he was connected to the emergency operator, explained Amelia's situation, and relayed her address. Once he was assured they were on their way, he turned to her. "What do you want me to tell Lukas?"

"Don't call him yet."

"Amelia, he ain't going to be happy to find out you didn't let him know about your accident. I bet he could get here before the ambulance leaves."

She shook her head again. "*Nee*. If you call the mill, it's going to send Luke and Rebecca into a dither. They'll come running over and take charge. I'm not ready for that yet."

Everything inside him disagreed with her. "They are going to worry."

"I know. But canna you contact them after we get to the hospital? That's not too long to wait."

Though he still didn't feel right about it, he didn't argue. She was in pain and she was also his weakness. He hated to refuse her anything. "The ambulance will be here soon. What do you need from the house?"

Relief filled her blue eyes. "*Danke*, Simon. All I need is my purse. It's on the kitchen counter."

"I'll be right back. You sit tight." Then he went to put a pouting Princess in one of the empty horse stalls and Oscar back in the house.

Unable to help himself, Simon wrote Lukas and Rebecca a brief note. He'd just finished it when he heard the sirens.

After grabbing her purse, he rushed back to her side. When she gazed up at him, her pretty eyes shining with unshed tears, he attempted to smile. "As you can tell, the ambulance is almost here. They'll take you to the hospital and give you something for your pain."

She still looked agitated. "Simon, I'm afraid," she admitted. Looking ashamed, she whispered, "The . . . The hospital brings back many bad memories."

"I know it does." He'd been in the same hospital waiting room when she'd learned that each of her parents had died. ▶

**A Sneak Peek** *(continued)*

"Would you go with me?"

"Of course." He almost groaned. Was she truly that oblivious to his feelings for her? "I'm not going to leave your side, Amelia. You couldn't get rid of me if you tried."

Her bottom lip trembled as she attempted to smile. *"Danke."*

"Never thank me for something like this. I don't want to be anywhere else."

She smiled as she pushed back some stray strands of her white-gold blond hair from her face. Only Amelia could look beautiful at a time like this.

He smiled at her again before walking out the barn door and waving to the ambulance approaching.

"She's in here!" he called out when one man and one woman opened the doors to the vehicle.

As he watched them get out a stretcher, Simon realized that he had now made his choice. He was done thinking of other people. He was done biding his time.

"Are you a relative?" the man asked.

"Boyfriend," he replied. Not even caring that it wasn't technically the truth.

As far as he was concerned, she would be his girl soon enough. He wasn't going to have it be any other way. ∽